Books by Allan W. Eckert

The Great Auk
A Time of Terror
The Silent Sky
Wild Season
The Frontiersmen
The Dreaming Tree
The King Snake
The Crossbreed
Bayou Backwaters
Wilderness Empire
In Search of a Whale
The Court-Martial of Daniel Boone
Blue Jacket
The Conquerors
The Owls of North America
Tecumseh!
Incident at Hawk's Hill
The HAB Theory
The Wading Birds of North America
The Wilderness War
Savage Journey
Song of the Wild

Song of the Wild

Song of the Wild

ALLAN W. ECKERT

Little, Brown and Company   *Boston*   *Toronto*

F

FIRST EDITION

LIBRARY OF CONRGESS CATALOGING IN PUBLICATION DATA
Eckert, Allan W
  Song of the wild.
  SUMMARY: A young boy's remarkable ability to
transfer his consciousness at will into any living
organism and to share what it experiences proves to
be an exhilarating but bittersweet gift.
  [1. Extrasensory perception — Fiction]
I. Title.
PZ4.E192So [PS3555.C55] 813'.54 [Fic]
ISBN 0-316-20877-9   80-15633

BP

Designed by Susan Windheim
Published simultaneously in Canada
by Little, Brown and Company (Canada), Ltd.

PRINTED IN THE UNITED STATES OF AMERICA

To my good friends . . .
Marge and Bob Schuttler

The author wishes to express his sincere gratitude to Dr. Norman Cornelius, DVM, of Arlington Heights, Illinois, both for his time, cheerfully given, and his very generous assistance in providing pertinent information for this book in respect to practices and procedures in the science and practice of veterinary medicine.

Song of the Wild

Chapter 1

"Answer me!"

The words were tight with poorly constrained irritation and the boy jerked his head around, nearly dropping the hoe. His brow furrowed with unaccustomed wrinkles and he felt his stomach muscles tighten with the realization that once again, unknowingly, he had angered his father. Caleb wished desperately he had heard the question for which an answer was being demanded and dredged his mind for any residue of the words still lingering, as a clue to how he should respond, but there was nothing.

"I'm sorry, Dad." He lowered his eyes. "I didn't hear what you asked."

Warren Erikson stood looking at his son in annoyance. The muscular arms crossed over his chest were tanned almost to the color of his velour pullover. His legs were slightly apart, feet firmly planted in the soil. The creamy suede shoes looked out of place in the freshly turned earth and the side of one was darkly smudged. Afraid this would irk his father even more, if he followed his son's gaze and saw the stain, Caleb looked up again, facing him directly.

"I'm sorry," he repeated softly.

"Sorry! You're always sorry, aren't you?" He paused, but the question was rhetorical and Caleb said nothing. In a moment Warren continued, less sternly but his voice still frosted with frustration. "I don't understand you. It seems every time I say anything to you, you're off in some never-never-land out there," he swept out an arm in a broad gesture, causing Caleb to flinch, "and too preoccupied to answer. Do you have any idea what you look like when you get in such a state?"

Caleb shook his head.

"Well, then, I'll tell you." The elder Erikson was warming to his subject. "You just stand there with your mouth open and your eyes blank, looking idiotic!" He shook his head. "It's no wonder people are talking about the way you act." He expelled a great gust of air and shook his head again, his conviction renewed that they should take Caleb to see a psychiatrist, despite the fact that Iris still objected. "I've tried to be patient with you," he went on, "tried to make allowances. But I'm telling you now that you just can't go on this way. Do you understand what I'm saying?"

"I understand."

The fire seemed to go out of the man and he relaxed faintly. "I hope so. Anyway, I'll ask you again — are you nearly finished out here?" At Caleb's nod he smiled and squeezed his son's shoulder gently, atoning through the gesture for the agitation he had exhibited earlier. "Good boy. I'm glad. Your garden's looking fine, just fine." His tone was lighter, but the words perfunctory. Neither Warren nor Iris Erikson had much real interest in vegetable growing, but they approved of Caleb's fascination with it and had not been disturbed at having a sizeable portion of the back yard usurped by Caleb's garden.

"Reason I'm asking," Warren went on, his hand still resting on Caleb, "is because after dropping your mother off over at the Blakeleys' for some sort of neighborhood chit-chat, I'm driving on down to Greenwood's to have the car checked out before we go on our trip. How'd you like to come along?"

Greenwood's was a Chevrolet sales and service dealership in Waukegan, five miles south, where Warren had purchased their station wagon last year. Had his father suggested that just he and Caleb share a walk along the Lake Michigan shoreline or in the woods at Kellogg Ravine just north of Zion, Caleb would have accepted the invitation eagerly. But now, because it seemed to the boy that he was being invited to go along simply as an afterthought rather than because Warren really wanted his company, he merely shook his head.

"No. I told Mike I'd play ball with him as soon as I got finished here."

His reply was colder than he'd meant it to be and he was honest enough with himself to realize that part of his reaction was inspired by his father's offhand reference to "our trip." It was a trip from which he was being excluded.

The tone of the reply had not been lost on Warren. His

lips tightened and his hand left Caleb's shoulder. Only a trace of slightly forced geniality lingered in his voice as he shrugged and replied. "Your choice. I told your mother you'd probably have something better to do. Okay. See you later. Be sure you're home by dinner time."

He spun around and strode swiftly back toward the house, brushing off one side of the crisp beige gabardine slacks as he walked. Caleb watched him go, remembering the cottontail rabbit he had been inhabiting when his father appeared a short while ago and wishing he hadn't had to leave it so quickly. The rabbit had squeezed through a hole in the chicken-wire fencing around the garden plot while Caleb had paused to rest, leaning against his hoe. Immediately upon seeing the animal, the boy had transferred his consciousness into it and reveled in the sensations that had followed. Unafraid of the motionless form of the boy, the rabbit had hopped to the neat rows of peas, beans, carrots, beets and other vegetables sprouting like green exclamation points from the rich-smelling earth.

In that instant of transference, Caleb had become one with the rabbit, experiencing with utter clarity whatever the rabbit experienced and abruptly finding himself in a wholly different world. He shared a momentary initial wariness with the rabbit as its keen hearing, smell and sight sought to detect possible danger, and he felt the bunching of the muscles as the animal hopped to the sprouts and began to feed. It had become obvious to him at once that the rabbit was a female. Through her nostrils the scent of the pea shoots was incredibly inviting. He had felt her head dip and the chisel-like incisors snip off a sprout at ground level, and had shared the movements of her tongue as it worked gradually to draw in the morsel, thrusting it between methodically grinding molars. The sprout had been crisp and juicy and, to Caleb, the crunching of the fibers was most reminiscent of chewing on raw celery; yet the taste he experienced through the sensors on the rabbit's tongue was far more exquisite.

This ability to penetrate the consciousness of the rabbit, or any other living creature for that matter, and experience whatever it experienced, was a talent that Caleb thought of with a special term. It was a term he had adapted from an off-hand comment his mother had made a year or so ago. On that occasion his parents were discussing him, unaware that he was in the next room and could hear them, and his father had expressed a growing impatience at Caleb's preoccupation with animal behavior.

"Does it really matter all that much?" his mother had responded. She had not yet reached the point where her son's affinity for nature had begun to bother her. "Actually, I think it's rather nice that he's developing such insight about nature."

The word insight had struck Caleb with considerable impact. It described quite well what he felt when he transferred into another living thing, and the play on words amused him. It was insight all right, with special emphasis on the "*in*." From that point on he had thought of his special talents as *in*-sight.

The rabbit was the latest of the scores of animals he had entered with *in*-sight and, lost in the delights of sharing the rabbit's experiences, he had also lost track of time.

More than two dozen vegetable sprouts had been ingested by the rabbit when she became alert at the sound of a door closing and footfalls approaching. With Caleb's conscious-ness still inside, she fled, plunging back through the hole and then swiftly along a faint trail canopied by the deep grass of which it was formed. Within thirty yards the ex-citing run had ceased and she settled herself over a small cup-shaped depression in the ground where, well camou-flaged, her four infants waited. As soon as she pressed her underside down over them, the tiny rabbits had begun to nurse and the sensation for Caleb was one of great plea-sure. It had been at this juncture that the boy had volun-tarily sent his consciousness back to his own body, only to turn and find that his father had been addressing him.

Now, pushing the memory aside, Caleb saw his father stop briefly beside the garage, call out something toward the house and flick his handkerchief at his shoe to clean it. Iris Erikson, slim and carefully dressed in a casual way, emerged from the back door, waved and blew a kiss in her son's direction and then vanished around the garage with Warren. In a moment the engine of the station wagon rumbled to life and quickly faded as the car turned from their driveway onto Edina Boulevard and drove off.

Caleb returned to his hoeing, concentrating closely on his work and refusing to let himself be sidetracked by a huge bumblebee droning past on ridiculously tiny wings, or by the female cardinal that momentarily alighted on the fence, swooped down to snatch up a small insect from the newly turned soil, then bounced away in erratic flight. He knew only too well what would happen if he let his attention be taken by such occurrences: He would feel himself drawn to them, joining them, as had happened with the cottontail and so many other creatures in the past, and his job would not get finished. So he shut his eyes and ears to their enticements and attacked the remaining unhoed ground in a flurry of activity, noting but not greatly caring about the missing pea and bean sprouts. He could plant others to take their places.

In another quarter-hour he was finished and left the vegetable patch after repairing the break in the fence, closing the gate behind him to keep out the rabbits. There were plenty of other things for them to eat without further onslaughts against his crops. He deposited the hoe in the toolshed attached to the garage and then stood in momentary indecision. Mike was expecting him, but he decided against going to his friend's house right away. It was just too nice a day to spend it all on ball-playing, with too many springtime things happening in nature that he might be able to share.

Caleb ambled diagonally across the street and entered the small Edina Park. He headed for one of the benches but, hearing a sound, stopped before reaching it. A group of fifteen or twenty redwinged blackbirds swept into view, wheeling and dipping in unkempt formation, and he could not resist. He willed himself into a fine male bird near the center of the flock.

It was difficult during *in*-sight for Caleb not to feel that he had, in fact, *become* the bird, since every sensory occurrence for the bird was shared equally in the boy's consciousness. Only the constant awareness of his total inability to control the bird's movements or motivate it to do anything it was not planning to do kept Caleb aware of his own consciousness within the bird. Nevertheless, instantly upon entering the blackbird he felt the rush of air flowing past and heard the beat of his own bird's wings and those of other birds surrounding him. The handsome scarlet epaulets on his bird's shoulders flashed, brilliant in the sunlight. He heard a barely audible twittering from some of the birds around him and felt the beak of his own bird open slightly, the twittering that emerged blending with the others. A faintly different call came from one of the other birds and at once his own tail flared, his right wing dropped and recovered. All around him the birds had flared similarly on the same wingbeat and the entire flock dipped and turned as one.

As the bird he inhabited soared, so too did Caleb's consciousness, exulting in the freedom of flight, in the glory of pumping wings, in the headiness of veering near and past outstretched tree limbs studded with newly unfurled leaves. The flock angled downward, rushed along mere inches above the grassy park surface, flowed easily over a bench and around a massive, gnarled tree trunk, then through an opening in a tangled hedge of multiflora rose and out across the expansive cattail marsh between the town and Lake Michigan. New reed spears were at half-height through the drab windswept remains of last year's stalks. A short distance ahead, other blackbirds rose in a cloud. The incoming birds intercepted and merged with them.

Now they were several hundred strong and still they moved as a unit, reacting sometimes to shrill cries by turning together simultaneously, and at other times, though reacting to nothing audible or visible, moving in synchrony through a process inspired by a peculiar, almost electrical impulse to which Caleb could not adjust his human thinking — an imperative beyond any means of communication he understood.

The bird Caleb inhabited abruptly broke away from the main flock, set his wings and sailed down toward where a cluster of bedraggled cattail spikes, shredded and faded and disreputable from the past winter's ravages, still projected from the water on stiff dried stems. He felt the feet of the bird thrust out with perfect timing, felt them touch and then grasp the soft broken top of a cattail. The dried plant swayed and creaked with the impact and the redwing's tail and wings spread and flicked as balance was expertly maintained until the movement ceased.

Other birds were landing close by on similar cattail spikes, as well as some on bent-over leaf spears which rustled and crackled at the unaccustomed weight. A female, much smaller than the male Caleb was occupying, alighted only inches away and ruffled her feathers as she looked with pretended indifference in another direction. Compared with the male, she was rather nondescript in appearance. Through the male's eyes, Caleb could see drab browns in overlying patterns on her back, and her breast was dun-colored with darker brown stripings. She had none of the male's splendid glossy blackness, nor the beautiful eye-catching shoulder patches of intense red bordered on the bottom by bright yellow. Even her beak was brownish-drab instead of the crisp black of the male's. Yet the male was intensely attracted by her. Caleb experienced the bird's movements as he preened himself into even greater splendor, running certain feathers of back and wings and breast through his beak, straightening ragged ribbings on the pinions and carefully readjusting the whole plumage for an appearance of elegance.

Caleb felt muscles tense as the male stretched himself to full length on the unstable perch, felt the wings open slightly and the feathers fluff until the bird's size was increased by half. He felt the head tossed back and the beak opened wide and he reveled in the pure melodious warbling which erupted from deep in his bird's throat. At that the female bird deigned to cast a brief glance in his direction, but still with the appearance of being singularly unimpressed.

The male redwing's feet tightened on the cattail and a bit of fluff from the spike tore loose, drifting away on a vagrant eddy of breeze. Caleb felt the head dip and the beak wipe back and forth across the fluff at the bird's feet, as if this were a process of tuning a delicate musical instrument to fine pitch. Once again the head was thrown back and Caleb experienced the vibrations in the throat as the warbling resumed.

"Hey, Cay! What's the matter? How come you're standing here like this? You all right? *Caleb?*"

At that, Caleb found himself back in the park, his upper arm gripped and being shaken vigorously by Mike Marlett. He turned and looked at his friend. "It's okay, Mike. I'm all right. I was just . . . listening to a bird singing."

"Bird?" Mike ran a grubby hand through scraggly red hair and frowned. The boy had a slight harelip but it was no impediment to his speech. "You must have pretty good ears. I sure didn't hear any bird. I went over to your house but you weren't there and then I saw you here from over there and you never even moved till I walked right up and shook you. But I sure never heard any bird singing."

"Okay, so you didn't hear it. I did. It was a bird singing, that's all — pretty far away, and I was just trying to stay still and hear it, that's all."

"I don't know, Cay." Mike shook his head, still frowning. "Lots of people are thinking you're sort of odd. Some of the guys're saying you're . . ." He broke off and made a spiraling motion with a stiff finger at one side of his head.

It was an attitude that Caleb had encountered a great many times in the past and, though it had made him uncomfortable and caused him to become progressively more secretive about his special ability, it had never upset him sufficiently to make him even consider not indulging in what he could do.

For a long time, when he was younger, Caleb had not known that other people could not project their consciousnesses as he did. He had hoped to encounter others who had this same ability, even if to a lesser degree. But he never had; and, as time passed, he began to realize that not only was his peculiar talent unique, there were times when it could become a distinct liability. He began to become fearful of mentioning it because the more he did so, the more he was ridiculed and made to feel he was stupid, a liar or very strange. People simply had no inclination to understand. Worse yet, in recent years he had found that people became suspicious and afraid of things they did not understand. Such fear and suspicion had a way of turning into hostility.

Now, facing his friend, Caleb replied defensively. "I

don't really care what people think, Mike." He cocked an eyebrow at his friend. "*You* don't think I'm crazy, do you?"

Mike placed a finger to his temple and furrowed his brow in exaggerated contemplation and then both of the boys burst out laughing. Mike pulled up his sleeve and looked at the Mickey Mouse wristwatch that Caleb had given him last Christmas. The crystal was cracked now and foggy with minute scratches, but it still kept good time. He snorted and playfully punched Caleb's shoulder.

"C'mon, bird-watcher, the guys are waiting."

The red-headed boy set off at a run, heading toward Edina Boulevard. The ball diamond at East School was three blocks south and two west. Caleb stood still a long moment, the experience within the redwinged blackbird still strong in him. Then he turned.

"Wait up, Mike," he yelled, breaking into a run.

Chapter 2

CALEB REHEARSED his excuse during the run home in the gathering dusk, knowing all the while that whatever he said would have little effect. He was nearly an hour late and groaned aloud as he ran. The ball game had gone into extra innings. It was this that he was all set to blurt when he burst in, sweating and panting, but there was no opportunity.

"You're late, Caleb." Ill-disguised anger lurked behind his father's level words as he put down his fork and swallowed the food in his mouth. "I told you to be home by dinner time."

"I —"

"No excuses, please. I don't want to hear them. Just get your hands washed and come to the table. Your mother held dinner for half an hour before we started. Is that any way to treat her?"

Abashed, Caleb slipped quietly past them at the table

and into the bathroom off the hall. As he washed hurriedly, he could hear the murmur of their voices but could not make out what was being said. When he returned and slipped into his chair, they were eating silently, their meal nearly finished. His own plate was filled and waiting. Although not very hungry, he began eating at once, staring at his plate and conscious that they were looking at him.

"How'd your game go, Caleb?" Iris asked. "Did you win?"

He shook his head. "We lost, Mom. Four to three."

"Oh, isn't that a shame." Her voice was gentle and he knew she was saying more than just those words; she was saying, "Your Dad's irked, honey. Just hang in there and he'll get over it as he always does," and he loved her for it. Somehow she always seemed to understand, and he was grateful for her presence. He ate quietly for a while and then looked up at his father, determined to make amends.

"Dad, I'm really sorry. I knew it was getting late and I should've come home. It's just that . . ." His words petered out and he dropped his gaze to his plate again.

"Tied in the ninth?" Warren smiled and there was no trace of irritation remaining.

Caleb nodded eagerly, brightening. "Uh huh. We lost it in the top of the twelfth."

"I guess that's understandable enough," Warren said, winking at his son. "You couldn't very well walk away before it was over." He took a sip of his coffee and continued while holding the cup. "Must've been a pretty exciting game."

"I hit a homer," Caleb blurted. "But we still lost."

"That's too bad." Warren was sympathetic. "Well, at least you tried. Better eat now so we can get things put away."

Caleb nodded and took another forkful of macaroni and cheese, paying little attention as his father began telling Iris about the work that had been done at the garage to correct the shuddering he had detected in their station wagon. The boy glanced at his mother, saw that she was looking at Warren, nodding at all the proper places and appearing to be listening to him. To the contrary, he knew she was not really hearing his father, any more than she heard her son when he rattled on about his experiences with animals. How could she be so loving and so sympathetic about so many things, yet still be able to turn off her mind like this?

The thought drew Caleb up short and he wondered if, in his own way, he were not much like his father — always rambling on about things that really interested no one, yet convincing himself that everyone was as interested as he. And if he *were* that way, would it become even more pronounced as he grew older? He didn't care very much for the idea and shook his head, then glanced up again, wondering if his parents had noticed the movement. They hadn't, and Caleb felt suddenly ashamed of himself. He loved his father and mentally chastised himself for his train of thought, feeling that in most respects he'd be fortunate to grow up to be like Warren Erikson.

His eyes shifted from his father to his mother, who held a coffee cup poised to her lips. He smiled faintly, liking the way a little tendril of the ash-blond hair had fallen into a half-curl over her forehead. At thirty-eight, Iris Erikson could not be termed beautiful, but she was still a nice-looking woman. Her jaw was perhaps a shade too angular, and the high cheekbones on occasion imparted a somewhat Asiatic aura to her expression. Her large eyes were as clear a blue as his own, bluer than the more steely coloration of Warren's.

The boy's father was pleasant looking, average in height, with sandy hair and a dependable and solid air. He had planned on going to college, but his father had died while Warren was in business college, and so he had taken over the Erikson Hardware Store and was now a well-respected member of the Zion business community. Both Iris and Warren loved this small city of Zion, nestled on the shore of Lake Michigan some forty miles north of downtown Chicago. Along with the hardware store, Warren had inherited this large old house on Edina Boulevard, where he had grown up. It was no grand estate, but neither was it one of the scattered cracker-box moderns that had sprung up on the town's periphery in recent years. Like Warren, it was solid and dependable, and it suited the Eriksons just fine.

It was in this very house that Caleb had been born a dozen years ago, and the old fashioned little city with its population of around eighteen thousand was the only place he really knew well. Zion, as its name suggested, had been founded by theocrats, and its principal north-south streets were named after Biblical figures — Gilead, Gideon, Ezra, Bethel, Enoch, Elisha, Elim and Edina. However, the fact that the Eriksons' son had been christened with a name having Biblical connotation had nothing whatever to do with the town. Caleb was simply a name that both Warren and Iris liked very much and found to be refreshingly less ordinary than most boys' names of the day.

The conversation between Caleb's parents had shifted to a casual discussion about whether or not Warren should run for a seat on the Zion city council, as others were urging him to do. Caleb sat quietly at his place, toying with his food and eating little, paying scant attention to their conversation. He was thinking of the redwinged blackbird and the flight he had shared with it to the marsh, reliving the ecstasy of hurtling through the air and plunging, rising, turning and landing in concert with those around him. The memory was nearly as good as the actuality and he was so lost in his thoughts that he gave a little start when his father reached over and touched his arm, then pointed toward the plate.

"You're not eating much," he said. "Feeling low over losing the game?"

For an instant the boy did not comprehend what his father was talking about. Then he shook his head. "No, I wasn't even thinking about it. I don't really care that we lost."

"What *were* you thinking about, dear?" Iris asked. She was sitting with her elbows on the table, fingers interlocked and her chin resting on them, looking at him steadily, curiously.

"Probably about summer vacation coming up and the good time he's going to have at Spring Hill Farm," interjected Warren, grinning. "About all I could think of when I was his age and school was so close to being out for the summer was vacation. I never spent one at a horse farm, though, and I have to admit I'm a little envious."

"No, that's not what I was thinking about, Dad," Caleb replied. "I mean, I'd much rather be going around the world with you and Mom than to that farm where I don't know anyone. But that's not what I was thinking about."

Over the past month, the matter of the trip had become a sore point. For years his parents had talked of taking a trip around the world: a trip scheduled to last all summer, with stops in many of the exotic places both of them had always wanted to see. Up until now it had always been put off for one reason or another. At first they had been reluctant to leave Caleb; later, they had worried about the inconvenience of taking a small child on such an extended trip. Now, however, it had become important for Warren and Iris to share this trip with no one. It would be the first time since Caleb was born that they would really be alone together. Both felt strongly that they needed to become reacquainted and that the trip would be, in essence, a sort of second honeymoon. Their relations with one another were not so much strained as they were undergoing an erosive sense of staleness, a reality of which they were becoming keenly aware and which disturbed them both considerably. They felt confident that a long trip alone together would revitalize them and their marriage. Perhaps next year they could take another trip and then Caleb would accompany them. But not this time. At age twelve, their son could now be left under supervision. Suitable arrangements had already been made.

Though he tried to hide it, Caleb was deeply disappointed at not being included in their exciting plans. The disappointment also created within him a sense of guilt he could not quite understand, reasoning only that he must have done something very wrong and this resulted in his exclusion. Their attempts to explain — without unduly alarming him about the stability of their marriage — were incomprehensible to him; he felt he was being punished and he didn't know why. And so his disappointment and guilt evolved into a strong resentment which occasionally manifested itself in terseness.

Now, at Caleb's reply, Iris looked concerned and she gave Warren a knowing look. He responded with a small shrug, not really having an answer at this point and tossing the ball back to Iris. She sighed and looked back at Caleb.

"Darling," she began, "please try to understand. It's not that your Dad and I object to having you with us. It's just that we're going to be gone quite a long time — practically all summer — and most of the things we're going to see and do simply wouldn't be very interesting to a twelve-year-old. You'd be bored and unhappy and that would make us unhappy, too.

"Everything's been arranged for you to stay with Judy Boyle," she went on, "and I know you'll have a wonderful time at Spring Hill Farm. You've never had a chance to be close to horses before and see how they're trained for jumping and all. I know you'll love it. You really will!"

"But I don't even *know* her," Caleb protested. "What if she doesn't like me . . . or if I don't like her?"

Iris laughed brightly. "Well *I* know her," she said, "and I guarantee you'll like her a great deal. I don't know of anyone who doesn't. She's one of the kindest and most generous people I've ever met. You remember I told you she was my closest friend in high school?"

Caleb nodded, recalling how, a few months ago, Iris

had come home from a shopping trip to downtown Chicago, hugely excited about accidentally running into Judy Boyle, with whom she had lost contact shortly after graduation from high school. Caleb and his father had listened with interest that night as she told them of the unexpected reunion. Judy, after high school, had gone to college in California and, being a poor correspondent, they had lost touch with one another. After two years on the West Coast, she had met and married Tom Boyle, a professional horseman. Within another year they had established Spring Hill Farm in Algonquin, Illinois, only thirty-five miles west and south of Zion. A riding school and boarding and training barn for show thoroughbreds, it had now become one of the more prestigious stables in the state, with many blue-ribbon horses.

All this had been related to Iris by Judy as they spent the afternoon together, both of them overjoyed at reestablishing their friendship, bringing each other up to date on their lives and both embarrassed at having failed to look one another up during the intervening years. Less than a year ago, Tom Boyle, though only entering middle age, had abruptly died of a heart attack. Since then Judy had run the operation alone. She had told Iris of how, during summers, she and Tom had often taken in orphan children to give them the experience of living in a home and learning about a horse farm for a few months, allowing them to help out with many of the menial tasks that were required to keep the operation running smoothly. It had worked out very well.

The discussion had inspired Iris to tell Judy of the tentative plans for the 'round-the-world trip during the coming summer and their concern about what to do with Caleb. They had been considering several different summer camps but as yet had not found any that was ideal. That was when Judy had suggested that Caleb be allowed to come and stay with her over the summer. The idea appealed to Iris enormously — and to Warren as well when he learned of it — and the details were firmed up by telephone over the next few weeks. Several tentative plans for driving to Algonquin with Caleb and giving Judy and their son a chance to get acquainted had fallen through. Now, with only a week of school remaining for Caleb, and with his parents' departure for Europe scheduled immediately after that, it was obvious that the boy and the horse farm owner would not meet until Caleb was taken there to be dropped off for the summer.

"Caleb, don't frown so," Iris continued now. "I know it would have been better if it had worked out so that we all could have gone to the farm for a visit first, but it just didn't happen. Everything'll work out fine."

Caleb made no response and Iris looked again at Warren in mute appeal. He cleared his throat and said, "You know your mother's right, don't you, son?"

"I guess so." There was a decided lack of conviction in the response. Warren chewed momentarily at his lower lip and then decided to change the subject. "A few minutes ago you were pretty much steeped in thought, but it wasn't about summer vacation or the farm, so what *were* you thinking about?"

The boy became uncomfortable. Too often before he had been unsuccessful in trying to explain to them his unique talent. At first they had listened with amusement only, considering his *in*-sight expeditions to be nothing more than the product of a fertile imagination. The amusement had quickly worn off as the trance-like periods gripped Caleb more often and he insisted more emphatically that he was truly able to project his consciousness into other creatures at will. Unable to countenance even the possibility of such a thing, they became concerned that he was escalating in his mind from acceptable make-believe to unhealthy prolonged fantasy. Their concern intensified when Caleb's odd behavior began causing neighbors or friends to view them askance or avoid the family entirely. Altogether too many of the people of Zion were beginning to add their own bits of fuel to the fires of rumor and suspicion about "that Erikson boy." There were some who even went so far as to consider the boy mentally defective. Among these was Caleb's seventh grade teacher, Arlene Olstrohm. Drawing upon a vast store of knowledge acquired during a one-semester course in abnormal psychology at Illinois State Teachers' College, she had expressed her opinion to the East School principal: "I believe Caleb Erikson suffers some sort of minimal brain damage, judging by the frequency with which he becomes dissociated."

The subject of Caleb's claimed ability became anathema in the Erikson household and he had long ago learned the inadvisability of trying to talk about it with his parents. It became one of the few subjects on which they simply could not communicate. Attempting to do so, Caleb knew only too well, had no effect other than upsetting them, resulting in their wrath descending upon him or in an ever-growing concern on their part that he actually did have a mental problem requiring the attention of a psychiatrist.

With this in mind, he was reluctant now to answer his father's question, abruptly repeated with a narrowing of his eyes.

"Well, I'd appreciate an answer, Caleb. What was it you were thinking of before?"

Caleb hesitated, not wanting to lie but finding himself forced into evasiveness. "I was . . . remembering about being in Edina Park today."

"Evidently you saw something in particular you were remembering?"

"Well, yes. I saw a big flock of blackbirds. Redwings."

Warren's frown deepened as he detected the evasiveness, but Caleb hurried on, hoping to divert the train of thought. "And I saw a mother rabbit, too. She was in my garden just before you came out there, Dad. And then, while I was in the park, Mike came and we —"

"A *mother* rabbit?" Iris interjected, cocking her head quizzically. "Did she have little bunnies with her?"

"No."

"Then how could you know it was a mother rabbit?"

"Well, . . ." he paused, realizing he was backing himself into a corner but not knowing how to extricate himself except by plunging on, ". . . she came through a little hole in the fencing and ate some of the pea and bean sprouts. Then," he shifted his gaze to his father, "she heard you coming, Dad, and ran off. I went with her. She went through a tunnel in the grass to a place where she had four little babies in a hole. She pressed down over the hole and started nursing them and —"

His father's suddenly upraised hand stopped him. "Wait a minute. You say she heard me coming and ran off and you went with her?"

Caleb nodded. "Uh huh. And she —"

"Why are you saying such a thing when you know it isn't true, Caleb?" his father interrupted, the words laced with disappointment.

"It *is* true!" The die was cast and Caleb knew that any further attempt to gloss it over would be pointless. He'd trapped himself and now must pay the price.

"Son, you're telling an outright lie and I have to tell you, I really don't like it a bit." His father was more saddened than angered as he continued with inexorable logic. "I had my eye on you from the moment I came out the back door and you never even budged. So how could you have followed a rabbit that was scared off by hearing me coming?"

Caleb's voice lowered to bare audibility. "I didn't actually *walk* after her. I just . . . well, sort of got inside her and went along."

The elder Erikson dropped his spoon into his saucer with a clatter and sat back, shaking his head. "That again! Make-believe. Haven't we gone that route with you often enough?"

"Warren, why do we always have to make such an issue of it?" Iris's voice was conciliatory, yet with a subtle sharpness, and she had raised her head. "He's just a boy. If he wants to pretend he's a rabbit, it's certainly not hurting anything."

"I wasn't pretending," Caleb flashed, louder than he had intended, his gaze shifting to his mother and then back to his father. He was incensed and frustrated at their disbelief; he knew that whatever he said now would make no difference, yet he was unable to restrain himself. "It *wasn't* make-believe. I put my mind inside her and went with her. I was inside her when she was eating and I went with her when she ran. And when she got to her nest where the babies were, I —"

"Not hurting anything?" Warren's words were flat and accusing, addressed to his wife. "You can listen to that sort of nonsense and say he's just a boy and it's not hurting anything?" His nostrils began to flare and he continued: "You didn't see him out there today the way I saw him, standing like a post in his garden, that blank look on his face, lost in that idiotic day-dreaming world of his somewhere! He does it all the time, Iris, and he's *got* to stop it and grow up. This isn't a dream world. This is here and now. Reality. And if he doesn't start getting a grasp on reality pretty soon, how's he going to be able to cope? God knows it's hard enough to get along when you're right on top of things!"

Iris opened her mouth to speak but Warren went on without pause. "And don't try to soften it by saying he's just a boy. He's twelve — nearly a teen-ager — and he'd better start paying attention to what's going on around him."

The rare anger flared more strongly in Caleb. "I *do* know what's going on around me — probably better than anyone else. I know things that are happening that nobody else knows about. Why can't you really *listen* to what I say, just once?" He caught himself up short, surprised at his own outburst, and his tone softened as he continued. "Dad," he said earnestly, "we've talked like this before a lot of times and I can't seem to make you understand. Please, *please*, just this once, try to understand that what I'm telling you isn't make-believe or daydreaming. It really happens. Honest! I really can get inside things and do what they do. I can —"

The crushing blow came then, not from his father but from his mother, breaking in softly but firmly. "Caleb, that's enough. I can understand your making believe these things are happening, but you *mustn't* try to convince us — or yourself! — that they're real. It's not healthy and your father's right. You've got to start paying more attention to reality."

"Mom!" Anger was giving way to anguish. "Won't you believe me? Please, won't you believe what I'm saying?" He looked back at his father. "Both of you? I'm not lying. It's true!" He felt tears springing to his eyes and blinked rapidly. "Why won't you just *listen* to me for once and try to understand what I'm —"

"That's enough!" Warren's flat palm smacking down on the tabletop rattled the dishes and silverware. "We're not going to sit here and listen to our own child tell us we don't understand him. We do, and we're only too well aware of what you're doing. So is everyone else in town. Now I want this silliness stopped. I mean it. You go on up to your room and think about it. You're grounded for the rest of the weekend."

Caleb glanced at his mother. She said nothing but her expression had softened and she reached out to pat his hand. He jerked away and left the room almost at a run, not stopping until he had slammed the door of his room behind him. He threw himself across the bed and lay there quietly, his feet hanging over the edge, hands gripping the spread fiercely, face buried in the material.

Below, he could hear his father's voice dimly. Warren was threatening to come up and punish him for slamming the door. The softer voice of his mother followed, the words too muffled to be understood but the tone conciliatory. His father did not come up the stairs.

Chapter 3

NOT UNTIL Iris Erikson sat down on the bed beside her son, gently smoothed his blond hair and touched cool lips to his cheek, did Caleb realize that he had fallen asleep and it was quite dark outside. The dim light on his small desk was shedding a friendly yellowish glow in the room.

"It's getting late, sweetheart," she said, kissing him again. "Better get undressed and clean up and then hop into your pajamas. You're all right, aren't you?"

He nodded, pleased that she had come to see him, yet with a faint anger still smoldering inside at her lack of belief. Her hand fell away from his head as he sat up on the edge of the bed, kicked off his shoes and began unbuttoning his shirt. She stood up and looked down at him, her features indistinct in the shadows.

"You didn't eat much of your dinner," she said. "I brought you a little snack." She indicated the glass of milk on the bedside table, beside which were two chocolate chip cookies on a paper napkin. "Your father and I are going to watch a late movie on television and then sleep a little longer in the morning." She leaned down and kissed him on top of the head and walked to the door, where she turned and looked back. "Be sure you shower and brush your teeth before going to bed. Good night, honey." She closed the door softly after her and he could not hear her go downstairs.

"Good night," he murmured.

He showered first and by the time he had put on his pajamas, eaten the cookies and drunk the milk, brushed his teeth and returned to his room, he was no longer the least bit sleepy. For a long while after turning off the light he lay on the bed with his arms crossed behind his head, staring into the semidarkness, watching the patterns of leaves from the oak tree outside as their shadows moved faintly on the wall across from the window, projected by the street light at the curb.

The sense of frustration was still heavy within him and he ached to be able to share his ability with someone. Though he had made the resolve before and found himself eventually breaking it, this time he swore to himself that he would never again mention his talent to them. He was utterly convinced now that they would never accept the actuality of it. He groaned faintly, feeling that if they really loved him, they would understand. Over the years they had become so inured to his excited, often seemingly interminable discourses about his experiences inside other living things, that there was no way that they could ever look upon it as anything but fantasy.

His own love of nature was intense and through *in*-sight his knowledge of how animals lived and what they did and felt was exceptionally advanced, augmented by his passion for reading — and remembering — whatever he could find in writing about natural history. Unfortunately, his burning interest in the subject was in no way shared by his parents. Warren Erikson's sole lifetime plunge into the study of nature had been a half-hearted attempt to assemble an insect collection when he was a high school sophomore — the success of which was evident in the fact that he barely passed the course. Iris Erikson's interest in nature was somewhat more developed, though hardly a passion. She could identify a robin when she saw one, or even a monarch butterfly, but she rather preferred to confine her natural history activities to occasionally pruning or repotting the several scraggly philodendrons or pothos that struggled for survival in large pots here and there throughout the house.

Along with his gnawing frustration, Caleb was deeply saddened by the knowledge that in their disbelief in him, both his parents were suffering a great loss, for he wished nothing more than to open a whole new wonderful world to them and they simply would not let him do so. Now he found himself yearning with almost palpable intensity to be able to open up to someone — *anyone!* — to be able to share this most remarkable of gifts. At the same time he was now, more than ever, fearful of divulging his ability to anyone ever again. He did not know how he came by the talent he possessed; only that *in*-sight was evidently abnormal and something of which to be ashamed, something that needed to be assiduously hidden.

Several times in the past Caleb had been tempted to tell Mike Marlett about it, but he had always held back, fearful of a scornful reaction even though Mike was his closest friend. If he could not convince his own parents of it, how could he convince Mike? Yet, because they were of the same age and very close, perhaps Mike might understand where an adult wouldn't. The more he considered it, the more the notion appealed to him, despite the little warning that sounded persistently far back in his mind that doing so could be a grave mistake.

His restlessness increased and he thought about reading the book he had begun yesterday after checking it out of the school library. It was William Beebe's *Edge of the Jungle* and he had become deeply absorbed in the scientist's penetrating observations of the South American flora and fauna. Caleb had half convinced himself that Beebe, with his remarkable insight into nature, must have shared, at least to some degree, the same talent he possessed of being able to project his consciousness into other organisms. The boy sat up and was reaching for the switch to his reading light when a faint scratching, fluttering sound stayed his hand. He stepped soundlessly to the window and saw, on the outside of the screen, a large cecropia moth clinging to the mesh with six furry rusty-red feet. Its broad wings were outstretched and faintly quivering. The cecropias, Caleb knew from his science class in school, were silk moths — the largest of all North American moths.

He moved quickly over to the desk, lifted the light-weight straight-backed chair to the window and sat down. With elbows resting on knees and his chin cradled in the heels of his cupped hands, his eyes were on a level with the moth. He studied it closely. The street light shed enough illumination for him to see the alternating red and white striping of the abdomen. The top of the insect's thorax was so heavy with a crop of the rusty-colored hair that it appeared to be a dense mane. Orange and white crescent-shaped eyespots on the wings broke the overall soft silvery-dusted light brown of the wings. At the tip of each of the upper wings, where the pale brown tapered off into creamy beige, there was a black eyespot half circled by a black crescent.

Caleb concentrated on the moth and simultaneously became one with it. Through the insect's multifaceted eyes he could see dimly past the screen to the hunched shadowy shape only inches away that was the boy with his chin resting in his hands. He could feel vibrations of the wings as minute muscles at the sides of the thorax flexed and relaxed with great rapidity, hastening the process of drying the tissues. Though the wings were outstretched and straight, a faint dampness remained on some of their surfaces, especially near the body. Only a short time before, Caleb knew, this moth had emerged from the cocoon in which it had been pupating and undoubtedly had crawled up the side of the house before pausing with a firm grip on the screen. The wings had been wrinkled and damp at emergence, but fluids pumped into them from the body had, like air blown into a crinkled balloon, caused them to stretch and straighten until now they were firm flat planes and all but dry.

The moth was a male, as evidenced by the huge feather-like antennae extending before the eyes. There was no sensation of hunger in the big insect, nor would there ever be. It possessed such reduced mouthparts they were all but nonexistent. Caleb was well aware that the species had been designed by nature to feed ravenously as a larva, but never as an adult. Its sole purpose during its life in mature form was simply to seek out a mate and fertilize her eggs before finally weakening and dying in a few days.

A faint breeze riffled the leaves, lifting one of the insect's wings momentarily, and Caleb felt the six feet automatically tighten their grip on the screening. Then the feet relaxed their hold, the powerful pectoral muscles put the wings into throbbing beats, and he was flying, fluttering halfway down to the ground at first until the initial inexperience was surmounted, then ascending rapidly until he was twice as high as the trees.

Below, the street lights of Zion formed criss-crossing patterns, merging in the center to the brighter glow of commercial lighting in the principal business district. Such artificial lighting held no attraction for the big moth. With his legs tucked up firmly against his body, the cecropia leveled off into a slower flight interspersed with moments of gliding, during which the wings were held at an angle of about thirty degrees from the body. Slight thermal currents caused him sometimes to rise or dip, but generally he held his altitude to about two hundred feet. In a short time the main part of the town was behind and it was darker below, but the moon was approaching full and, in its glow, even the cubical shapes of unlighted buildings below were visible.

As the moth flew, Caleb could feel the great antennae rising and lowering, turning, seeking, testing air currents for something that at first was absent. After several minutes it came, wafted by a faint tendril of breeze from the southwest — a peculiar, exciting, irresistible aroma caught by the acute sensors in the moth's antennae. Instantly the directionless soaring ceased and Caleb could feel the expansive forewings beating with greater purpose, the smaller hindwings angling to turn the moth on a course for following the elusive invisible spoor to its source.

A mile passed, then two. Not until nearly three miles had been traversed and the lights of Waukegan Memorial Airport were twinkling below did the cecropia set his wings at a sharper angle and slip downward. The scent was much stronger now, emanating from scrub growth lining the shores of a small drainage rivulet in the far southeastern quadrant of the airport. A stand of scrubby willows rose here, the frilly new leaves reflecting silver in the moonlight, and it was to the apex of the highest clump that the cecropia flew without hesitation. He alighted on a bare limb only a few inches from a female considerably larger than himself, her body parallel to a vertical broken twig projecting upward from the branch. Her trembling wings were outstretched to their full span of just over six inches and her abdomen — twice the size of his — was raised, the outermost tip emitting the powerful scent that had drawn the male from so far away.

The male cecropia, his own wings atremble, crawled somewhat clumsily along the branch to the upright twig, then upward on that until he was level with her at the top, on the opposite side. Seeing her close up through the eyes of the male, Caleb could now fully appreciate the size of the compound eyes — enormous convex black orbs neatly latticed into a multifaceted complex of individual lenses. The principal difference between the sexes, apart from her larger size in wings and abdomen, was the fact that her antennae, rusty-red and feathered like the male's, were only about a quarter the size of his. They moved and turned and were evidently picking up his aroma. They dipped and touched the male's antennae and a strong sense of pleasurable recognition flooded the male.

The female's two forelegs reached out over the outermost tip of the twig stub and touched the male. Caleb could feel this contact with yet another pleasurable surge, and the forelegs of the male he inhabited reciprocated. There was great satisfaction in the mutual touching. The scent from the female was overpowering, exhilarating beyond any words Caleb possessed, and he felt the abdomen of his host arch toward the female's and touch it at midpoint. Instantly hers lifted toward him and their tips touched, opened, connected. Strong claspers on each side of his posterior spread and gripped her, firmly locking them together.

The wing-trembling of both moths ceased as the connection became solidly seated. A peculiar secretion from one or both of them virtually glued them together. In moments there began a passage of seminal fluid from the male to the female, aided by convulsive contractions of his abdominal muscles. It was exhausting and the action could not be maintained. The contractions ceased, but still the insects remained connected, their wings hanging limply. For fully ten minutes they remained this way and then the contractions of the male resumed briefly. Again exhaustion followed in a minute or two and the activity ceased, except for a resumption of a brief touching together of forelegs and antennae.

Had they been uninterrupted, they might have stayed joined in this manner for many hours more, but another male sailed in from the darkness and landed at the base of the vertical twig. Immediately he crawled up to the pair and Caleb could feel the forelegs of the newcomer clutching at his host's body. Through the compound eyes he could see those legs were also grasping at the female, climbing over them both, trembling in excitement. The new male thrust his abdomen toward theirs without fulfillment and his efforts caused all three insects to flutter their wings to maintain balance. It was this excessive movement that attracted the attention of a predator.

In utter silence a huge shape landed on the branch on one foot, balancing itself with great flapping wings, while the other foot stretched out toward the trio. A wash of fear flooded Caleb's in-moth senses as, through his host's eyes, he saw the powerful foot touch the newcomer cecropia and grip. Sharp hard talons plunged through the soft body and drew the second male, fluttering wildly, to the lower branch. The screech owl's head dipped, taking the body of the moth into its mouth. With one snap of the beak, both the hindwings and forewings were snipped away. The four severed sections spiraled down into the darkness. The owl arched its body, stretched its neck and swallowed. The unfortunate male cecropia was gone.

Caleb felt the muscles of his moth tighten, drawing the wings together over the back and locking them in place. At the same time the feet relaxed on their perch and the male was jerked aloft, unresistingly being borne along backward by the female, who was flying strongly, their abdomens still adhering to one another. Strong though the wingbeats of the female were, she was considerably hampered by the unaccustomed weight of the male. It was a deadly drawback.

Facing backward as he was, the male cecropia caught a glimpse of the shadowy figure of the owl as it closed in, and fear thrilled through Caleb once more. He felt the wings of his host begin to work frantically. The claspers opened and the abdomen jerked to sever the connection binding him to the female, but to no avail. While in solo flight either moth might easily have outmaneuvered the owl and escaped, they could not do so in tandem. The screech owl overtook them easily.

As the owl hurtled past, one foot clawed out at them and Caleb experienced his host's pain as talons pierced the fleshy body. The impact tore male and female apart and instantly she vanished in the darkness, flying in a wildly erratic pattern. Whatever the fate of the male moth now, Caleb knew, his ultimate purpose in life had been fulfilled. The four hundred eggs within the female had been fertilized. With luck, over the next few days they would be lightly glued in groups of from two or three up to a dozen at a time on the foliage and twigs of willows or plums, apples, wild cherries, box elders or any number of the deciduous trees whose leaves provide food for the larvae of cecropias. In about fifteen days they would hatch and a new cycle would begin.

Even as the female escaped, the terrible pressure of the flying owl's clenched foot was crushing and incapacitating the male moth; and by the time the night hunter neared its chosen landing site on the broad lower branch of a giant oak, Caleb's moth was nearly dead. Its vision no longer functioned, the optical nerve fibers having been severed or crushed by a talon, and the formerly sensitive antennae were receiving nothing. With the life senses ebbing, all that remained was a deep, encompassing pain against which the punctured abdomen still twitched in spasmodic response.

It was at this point that Caleb transferred his consciousness to the owl.

Abruptly he could see again, very clearly. He could feel once more the flow of the night air past him; he experienced the strength of the owl's wingbeats and the possessiveness of clutching the prey in one foot. A dozen feet or more from the branch, the wings set and cupped the air, the short tail spread to full expanse, aiding in the braking action, and the free foot extended in anticipation of the perch. Forward flight nearly ceased as the owl reached the huge limb and, with a few expert strokes of the wings, it settled lightly to the rough-barked surface.

The screech owl was an adult female. Upon landing, she merely stood still a moment, gripping the wood with her free foot, bracing herself with the one holding her prey. The huge eyes blinked slowly a time or two, then, without haste, she bent her head and used her sharply hooked beak to snip off the moth's wings. She took the body of the moth in her mouth, jerked forward to toss it inside to her throat and swallowed. The juices that spilled in her mouth brought a sense of satisfaction and, after clicking her beak a time or two with loud snapping sounds, she bent over and rubbed the sides of it in succession against the bark to clean off any residue.

Caleb had never before entered the consciousness of an owl and the sensations he was experiencing through her were new and exciting and certainly very different. He reveled in the sensation of the feathers being fluffed to settle back into proper place any that had been disrupted during her exertions. Expecting her vision to be extremely clear in the darkness, he was somewhat taken aback at its limitations. Her sight now was not to be compared with his own sight by daylight. Although large objects could be seen fairly well at considerable distances, it was hardly with the degree of detail he had anticipated. The vision was especially limited when directed toward the ground where shadows were deep and Caleb wondered how the bird could detect prey. With a faint sense of disappointment, he suspected he was perhaps not experiencing the full degree of vision the bird itself possessed. If so, this would be the first occasion when he did not share full sensitivity with his host.

Having completed the cleaning of her beak and rearrangement of her plumage, the owl now leaped into flight and sailed to the topmost branch of a tall sapling that had died and was now a bare white skeleton rising from a fence row. In time it would decay at the base and fall to some gust of wind, as many of its branches had already fallen, but for now it was a good place from which to hunt, with the view unobstructed in all directions. Caleb suspected this was a favorite perch of the owl.

He felt her hunch down comfortably and slowly turn her head. Through her eyes Caleb could barely make out that on one side of the fence below was a meadow of thick grasses; on the other, the chopped-up remains of a soybean field from last year, the ground plowed, disked and harrowed, ready for planting. The ground surface was only dimly visible, and once more Caleb wondered how the owl could see any sort of prey — a mouse, for example — if it were to appear in either field.

For the first time he became aware of the bird's incredible sense of hearing. A variety of sounds were being received, some easily recognizable and some he had never heard before but which painted interesting pictures in his mind's eye. The honk of a car horn and the whirring of tires traveling at high speed on pavement came with startling clarity and the bird's head swiveled toward the sound. The nearest highway was fully three-quarters of a mile away and Caleb was amazed when he saw through his host's eyes the distant auto. There was no moving car anywhere closer, yet how could the sound have come so clearly?

A branch, long dead and brittle, snapped of its own weight and fell to the ground with a thud. The screech owl's head turned at the sound and her eyes looked toward a woodlot easily several hundred yards distant. They were the nearest trees to the dead sapling in which the owl perched, and the sound had not originated from beneath this tree. Again Caleb marveled at the acuteness of the owl's hearing.

More sounds came; strange slitherings and scratchings, chirps, faint whistles, the delicate pinging sound of a roving bat's sonar, the swish of grasses and rustle of leaves. Toward some of the sounds the owl would turn her head, toward others she did not respond. Caleb discovered that the whole head of the owl had to be turned for her to see a specific object. Unlike the eyes of other higher animals he had inhabited, hers were unable to be moved in their sockets; they were set to see forward only. This explained to Caleb's satisfaction the peculiar angles at which owls often held their heads. At one point a dog, trotting along through the dark field of prepared earth, approached the tree, and the owl locked her gaze on it instantly. As it came closer, the owl's head turned even farther, following its progress. As the dog passed behind the tree, the owl's head was swiveled so far around that she was looking almost straight down backward. At last she reached the limit of her head-turning ability and in the blinking of an eye snapped her entire head around, unwinding her neck and stopping with her gaze backward on the dog again, able now to continue moving the head to follow the canine's progress. The dog, never suspecting it was being watched, passed quickly from sight and eventually from hearing.

For a long while the owl dozed and there was little of interest to hold Caleb's attention. He contemplated leaving the bird, having been with her well over four hours. Considering that he had surely been with the cecropia moth for close to an hour before that, it was really time for him to be getting back within himself. Just as he was on the verge of doing so, the owl straightened and opened her eyes. There was nothing to see and little to hear and Caleb remained, wondering why she had roused. Within the bird's stomach he could feel a strange hardness, a discomfort demanding alleviation.

In conjunction with a convulsive hunching and a tightening of the abdominal muscles, the bird opened her mouth astonishingly wide and ejected a compact egg-shaped pellet of indigestible materials. The consciousness of Caleb recalled from things he had read that unlike many other birds of prey, which shredded victims with their beaks, eating the flesh and largely discarding fur, bones, feathers, chitin and other nondigestibles, the screech owl swallowed most of her food whole. During the process of digestion, all the material with food value had been assimilated into the owl's system, but the indigestible residue, now compacted into a tight oval pellet, was being regurgitated. Slick with stomach fluid, the pellet shot from the bird's mouth and fell to the ground with a tiny plop. A moment later the whole process was repeated with another pellet.

A dawning sense of hunger filled the owl, returning her to predatory alertness, and so Caleb stayed with her. A quarter-hour passed, then another, and the bird continued keenly alert. Sounds were sharp and clear again, and the bird directed her vision toward each one, then relaxed slightly to wait for another. At last, with the moon low on the horizon, there came a different sound. Caleb could feel the owl's muscles tighten.

The barely audible squeak was twice repeated. At the first, the owl's head snapped around and her vision was directed generally to a patch of the heavier pasture grasses perhaps a hundred feet or more from the base of the tree. At the second, she cocked her head so that more of the sound would be gathered by one ear than the other and instantly she took off. Her incredibly keen hearing had told her not only the direction from which the sound had emanated, but also its distance away to within a fraction of an inch.

As if sliding down a steep wire, the owl angled to the attack swiftly and in absolute silence. The third squeak came then, originating from a slightly different direction. The prey was moving, and in mid-flight the owl corrected her course accordingly, zeroing in on the one final sound — a faint leafy rustling from an area where a loose tangle of old branches lay.

The owl's wings were only two-thirds opened during the dive and as she plunged toward the tangle, Caleb shared the experience of two things happening: While wings and tail cupped for the braking action and both feet stretched far forward with talons widely outstretched, simultaneously a tough clear membrane closed over each eyeball just as the bird plunged into the tangled branches and grasses. This, Caleb knew, was the nictitating membrane. Though it cut down the limited vision considerably, there was still sight enough left to see and avoid large obstructions. A tiny twig, unavoidable in her plunge, poked against the owl's right eye and slid harmlessly off the pliable transparent membrane. Had the protection not been there, almost surely the eyeball would have been badly scratched, perhaps even punctured.

In the midst of the attack, Caleb suddenly understood that he had indeed been seeing with the owl's full vision and that she did not really depend upon her eyes for hunting anywhere nearly so much as she depended upon her ears. Prey was located and pinpointed by ear, while vision was used almost exclusively to avoid colliding with large objects. The screech owl dived through the maze of branches and into the grasses beneath. The instant her feet struck, she grasped fiercely.

A short-lived little shriek erupted and though the owl had never seen the mouse before her feet touched it — any more than the mouse had heard her approach — her remarkable hearing had permitted her to home in to the prey with deadly accuracy. The piercing talons quickly found the little rodent's heart and it stiffened in her grasp and died. She paused only long enough to regain her balance, grasp the mouse by the back of its neck in her beak and take off.

The powerful wingbeats carried her on a direct course to a large old willow growing at the southern outskirts of Zion. Upon reaching it, she landed on a thick branch just below a four-inch hole in the main trunk. For a moment she stood still, listening. Then, juggling the dead mouse momentarily in her mouth until she had it positioned head first, she threw back her head and devoured it whole in two convulsive swallows.

As before, she wiped her hooked beak back and forth across the bark at her feet, cleaning it meticulously. Then she preened her feathers, gently running the long pinions one after another through her beak. Looking at these flight feathers through her eyes, Caleb could see that the leading edges, instead of being hard and dense as in the feathers he had found shed by pigeons or crows or other birds, were soft and fluted like a miniature comb. It was this fluting that caught and muffled the wind in her passage, allowing her to fly in silence and thereby surprise her prey.

The owl's head turned slowly for one last look around before she retired. Then, with delightful grace and agility, she leaped upward and flitted to the hollow, balanced there a moment and then dropped inside. Though her eyes were open, Caleb could see nothing save the dim light of the night sky at the entry hole a few inches overhead. The feet were on a soft spongy material which Caleb took to be punky decayed wood bits. Fluffing her feathers a final time, the little owl hunched down, nestled her head snugly on her shoulders and closed her eyes. Within moments she was sound asleep.

Caleb knew he must delay his departure no longer. Even as the thought struck him he returned to his own bedroom. This was the longest he had ever remained away from his own body and he groaned faintly as he straightened in the chair, wincing at the deep indentations his elbows had made on his legs just above the knees. Nevertheless, he was very content with what he had experienced, and the earlier pain of the confrontation with his parents was no longer upsetting him.

Crossing back to his bed, he slipped between the sheets, thinking of the fascinating world he had just left and what a shame it was that he could not share it with his parents. Again the yearning was strong in him to be able to talk with someone and share these marvelous experiences. Once more the thought of Mike Marlett came to him and he was smiling as he fell asleep.

Chapter 4

DESPITE THE FACT that Caleb had not gone to bed until an hour before dawn, he was awake and dressed before eight o'clock. He felt refreshed and alert and was convinced that during *in*-sight the effect on his own body during the time he was gone was much akin to sleep. As he slipped downstairs, taking his empty milk glass with him, he passed the slightly ajar door to his parents' room and heard his father's faint snoring. Iris's bare left foot was sticking out from under the sheet that covered them. Caleb was reasonably sure they would not be up and about until after nine o'clock.

The large downstairs room that had originally been a drawing room when the house was built around the turn of the century had been converted by the Eriksons into a family room. The condition of the room attested to how late his mother and father had stayed up watching the Saturday night late movie. They had probably both become very sleepy because, while normally his mother would never leave the room messy, the ashtrays were full and used glasses were on the end tables, partially filled with a residue of melted ice. The small plates from which they had evidently eaten a late snack were on the coffee table, along with cups and saucers and a stainless steel thermal jug in which there remained a cup or so of tepid coffee. Warren's shoes were on the floor beside his big chair.

To make amends for being late coming home last evening, Caleb quietly cleaned the room and carried the dirty dishes to the kitchen where he washed them and put them away. He was still ebullient about last night's occurrences with the cecropia moth and the screech owl, enjoying the memories that came to him.

Since Caleb's unique ability to project his consciousness had always been a part of his life, there were certain creatures he had entered many times in the past, simply because he encountered them frequently. Often he had transferred into the consciousness of robins, sharing with them their flight, nest-building, egg-laying and rearing of young. He had experienced how they yanked nightcrawlers from the ground and fed them to clamoring nestlings. On occasion he had entered the nestlings themselves, or even the nightcrawlers.

More times than he could remember, Caleb had observed — through the senses of the animals involved — the actions of sparrows and grasshoppers, mice and turtles and toads. Once he had experienced the special thrill of projecting himself successively into members of a large migrating flock of mallard ducks, exulting in his participation in their strong flight and in the murmured quackings that passed among them. Another time he shared the ecstasy of soaring effortlessly on widespread wings as the huge red-tailed hawk he inhabited plied the thermal air currents with consummate skill.

He had often entered the consciousness of scurrying ants, sharing in their ceaseless labors, traveling with them through labyrinths of subterranean tunnels. Sometimes, especially in autumn, he had become one with a monarch butterfly, joining with many thousands of others as they clustered on trees and bushes in Illinois Beach State Park in preparation for their southward migration. Occasionally he had entered bees or wasps, beetles or centipedes, chipmunks or squirrels, tadpoles or frogs, horseflies, crickets, dogs, cats, goldfish, guppies, crayfish, snails, cicadas and a host of others. One time his parents had taken him to the Milwaukee Zoo. He had been thrilled at the opportunity to project himself briefly into tigers and giraffes, hippos and gorillas and elephants; but when he did so, the sensations were not at all good, the frustrations of the caged and otherwise confined animals so disturbing to him that after transferring briefly into only a few he could not stand any more and, much to the bewilderment of Warren and Iris, begged to go home.

From all the animals he inhabited, Caleb learned an impressive amount. He came to know their habits intimately; how they protected themselves, what they ate, how they mated, where and how they laid their eggs or gave birth, the mechanics of their walking, running, flying or swimming, how they dug beneath the ground or carved holes in trees, how they hunted or were themselves hunted. And as he collected such an enormous store of first-hand knowledge from the animals inhabiting the world of nature about him, he became appalled at how erroneous in their information were many of the books he read.

Less frequently, Caleb would enter trees and shrubs, weeds and vegetables, flowering plants, mosses and fungi. In their sensations he found minimal excitement, yet a profound sense of peace most animals never achieved. Nevertheless, he rarely stayed with any individual of the plant world for long, simply because their senses were more limited than those of animals and their experiences relatively unchanging. Once in a while, however, there were sensations he shared with plants that were extremely gratifying. This morning was one such time.

Although the sun had been shining brightly when he came downstairs and the sky above was a clear deep blue, there was a rolling buildup of heavy clouds far on the western horizon. By the time he had finished clearing up last night's debris and had a slice of coffee cake along with a glass of milk, the menacing clouds had blanked out the sun and an aura of impending storm filled the air. It was not unusual; thunderstorms often moved in with little warning. In the living room there was a large semicircular bay window with a curved window seat along its length upon which it was a delight to sit and look outside. It was here that Caleb positioned himself to watch the storm come in.

Rainfall had been slight this spring and the earth was dry, the new grasses less emerald than they might have been. The enormous old white oak in the front yard, its great trunk easily five feet in diameter, stood with young leaves hanging limply. Heavy gnarled limbs projected from the trunk and spread out to form a living umbrella over the house, driveway, front yard, sidewalk and even much of the street. An exceptionally fine old tree — which Iris steadfastly maintained had to be at least two hundred years old — each summer it produced a sizeable crop of acorns which attracted a number of bold fox squirrels living in the area. There were even a couple of leafy squirrel nests, larger than basketballs, in the upper branches and a deep hollow forty feet up the trunk where an aging, ill-tempered male squirrel lived. Caleb had entered the consciousness of that particular squirrel at least a score of times and he held a particular affection for it.

Overhanging the sidewalk, curb and part of the street was a large dead branch — a much resented reminder to Warren Erikson of one of his frequently postponed home maintenance projects. He knew he should cut it down before it fell of its own accord and possibly damaged something or hurt someone, but somehow he never quite managed to get around to doing it. On the side of the big tree facing the street, beginning at the base of the dead branch and running up the trunk for ten or fifteen feet, was an old healed-over scar where many years ago the tree had been struck by lightning, probably the cause of the large branch having died.

With the first muted rumblings of thunder in the distance, Caleb projected himself into the giant oak. There was nothing to see, since the tree had no organs of sight, yet there was a distinct sensitivity to light, as well as to air pressure. Caleb could feel the sagging weight of the thousands of leaves. Even as his consciousness centered on them, they began to move. Stirred to life by the freshening breeze as the storm front neared, they turned on their stems as if rousing from a deep sleep and began trembling in anticipation. They whispered to one another in rustling anxiety and turned their lighter-colored undersides windward.

The wind intensified and the branches themselves seemed to speak, whining and moaning with their movement, often rubbing against one another and groaning deep grumbling sounds as if protesting the disturbance. In a matter of minutes the groaning became a more agonized shrieking as the wind became a blasting force, whipping the tree with tremendous power, bending its more limber upper regions as if they were made of rubber. Even the mighty trunk swayed and creaked under the lashing fury, and Caleb felt the sap quickening in the fibers, coursing with greater vigor through the trunk and twigs and leaves.

Some of the weaker, less well-formed leaves ripped away and there was, if not a feeling of pain as Caleb knew it, at least a sense of minor injury and loss, not unlike the sensation of a single hair plucked from the head, but multiplied scores of times. There were little dead dry twigs interspersed with the limber living branches and their brittleness allowed no leeway for bending with the pressure of the gale; they snapped and whirled off with the storm. Both leafy squirrel nests tore loose from their anchorage and tumbled away, snatched by the greedy wind like great treasures stolen from a giant who was powerless to give chase.

The rain came then, sheets of it pounding down at a sharp angle and smashing with tiny wet force into leaves and bark. Miniature rivulets formed and coursed down the craggy bark, following the natural crevices as if they were ravines eroded from eons of rain running over the surface. Streams of water poured off the leaves, gouted from low-sweeping branches as from rain gutters, sped to the ground at the tree's base and splashed over emergent roots. Beneath ground surface the soil became damp, wet, saturated as the rainwater penetrated ever deeper, bathing thirsty rootlets with an elixir of life, refreshing and rejuvenating the mighty tree. Caleb could feel the moisture being absorbed through a vast network of rootlets and the very pulse of the tree quickening. He wanted the ancient oak to stretch mightily, wanted it to lash back at the wind, wanted it to whip the gale as the gale had been whipping the tree, but his own wishes and thoughts were of no consequence.

The storm reached peak intensity and with that came searing blue flashes of lightning and the whole earth vibrated with their power, tingling with electric thrill. A bolt smashed down with crackling intensity, striking a large branch near the oak's pinnacle, close to where it joined the trunk. The great tree screamed as its upper portion exploded in blinding, instantaneous heat and the odor of ozone briefly filled the air, then was whipped away. The whole top of the oak was severed in a splintered mass and crashed downward through the other branches, shoving some out of the way, taking certain smaller ones with it. The mass struck the huge dead branch overhanging sidewalk and street and it snapped with a tremendous crash and sprawled with the topmost portion onto the pavement.

There was fear then, and Caleb could not tell whether it was his own or a sense emanating from the tree. It was strong and debilitating, imbued with such terror that he was sure it must be his own; yet, didn't the grand old tree seem to brace itself even more? Didn't it seem as if the roots dug in deeper, thrusting widespread toes through the soil in an effort to hold on? The wind pressure was terrible and the whole tree leaned. Tiny rootlets strained and larger foundation roots heaved against the weakening soil.

And then it was over. The howling wind conceded its defeat and died to no more than an occasional ineffectual gust; splashing rain ceased and became a gentle, diminishing drizzle. The great tree settled back, seemed to relax, and there was the sensation that it shrugged heavy shoulders to scatter the loose residue of droplets still clinging. There was even the impression that the tree exhaled mightily, imbuing the surrounding air with its aroma of freshened, dust-free leaves and the pungency of wet bark.

Though injured, the ancient white oak was still standing. One day, perhaps, another such storm would come, when it would be even older and weaker, less able to withstand the onslaught, less resilient to the fierce wind, and it would topple at last. But not yet.

Caleb returned to himself and viewed the tree through his own eyes. There was a slight whisper of sound from behind him and at the same time he felt a hand come to rest on his shoulder.

"Our beautiful oak." The words were murmured sadly and he turned and smiled up at his mother as she continued. "Look what's happened to it, Caleb. Oh, it's such a shame."

He patted her hand. "It's okay, Mom. It's still standing. Only part of the top and that big dead branch over the street fell."

Iris was clad in a warm velour robe the color of sliced peaches. The collar was up and the robe was belted snugly about her waist, yet a chill swept her and she crossed her arms, hugging herself to still it. She looked at Caleb and smiled, cheered by his words. "Were you sitting here when the lightning struck? Lord, what a crack it made! At first I thought it hit the house."

He nodded, his own smile secretive. "I was here." He pointed out the window. "Look at what else happened, though."

Edina Boulevard was littered with an almost unbroken carpet of fallen leaves and branches. Two doors away, on their side of the street, a large elm tree that had been dying from Dutch elm disease had been blown down and lay across the Walkers' front yard, projecting over the sidewalk and effectively blocking the street. One of the larger branches that had struck first had severely gouged their picture-postcard lawn.

"Well," said Iris, "that certainly saves the Walkers the two hundred and fifty dollars the tree service said they'd charge to take that elm out. Barbara and Gordon'll have a fit when they see what's happened to their lawn."

Diagonally across the street, in Edina Park, there was another tree down. That one was a maple, not struck by lightning but evidently blown over as the Walkers' elm had been. In the park, too, the ground was well littered with a jumbled array of broken branches, many with leaves still attached.

During the remainder of the morning and much of the afternoon, the debris throughout town was cleared away. To the satisfaction of Barbara and Gordon Walker, a Zion municipal crew came in a large orange truck to dismember the big elm, cut it into lengths and haul it away. Caleb's father prevailed upon them to use their chain-link saws to cut the larger branches and upper portion of the trunk into lengths suitable for the fireplace. This was also done with the tree in the park and with both the top and the large dead branch from the Eriksons' oak. Warren gave the three workmen five dollars apiece and then he and Caleb made trip after trip to the back yard, stacking the logs alongside the garage. While they worked, Warren chatted amiably with his son and Caleb found a keen pleasure in sharing the work with his father. Warren was so impressed with the amount of work Caleb was doing that halfway through he paused, put his arm around his son's shoulders and hugged him.

"For doing such a good job here, Caleb, I'm going to give you five dollars when we're finished."

Caleb glowed. Just the uncommon closeness and praise were payment enough. Times shared like this had never occurred often enough to suit him.

In mid-afternoon they were joined by Mike, who had pedaled over on his bicycle to ask Caleb to go with him on a spin around the town to view the storm damage, but Caleb shook his head. "Can't go," he said. "I'm grounded."

Warren overheard and seemed on the point of rescinding the restriction, but then merely shook his head and moved toward the garage with another armload of wood. Mike discarded his idea and stayed with Caleb, helping to stack the remainder of the wood and earning a dollar for his efforts.

When they finished, Iris ruffled Mike's hair and hugged Caleb close. "I haven't had a chance to thank you for cleaning up the family room this morning," she told him. "That was very thoughtful of you . . . and terrible of me to have left it that way. Your Dad and I were so pooped we just couldn't stand the thought of anything except collapsing. Anyway, how 'bout you two coming inside for some milk and chocolate cake?"

The boys needed no coercing. After they'd snacked, the two went up to Caleb's room to play a game of Monopoly. Sprawling on the floor as they set up the game, Caleb looked across at Mike and felt a strong wave of companionship between them. Having convinced himself that Mike would neither laugh at him nor tell others what Caleb told him in confidence, he made his decision. He leaned conspiratorially toward the red-headed boy.

"Mike, I've got a terrific secret."

Mike looked up, immediately interested. "A secret?"

Caleb nodded and began carefully, ready to withdraw in an instant if he began feeling he was making a mistake. "You may not believe this at first, but it's true."

Impressed with Caleb's seriousness, the red-haired boy nodded again. "Okay. Tell me."

Caleb shook his head. "Not yet. I'll tell you, but only if you promise me you won't tell anyone else about it. I mean *anyone* — not your mom and dad, not Chuck or

Jack or Freddie or any of the guys at school. Not anybody."

Mike touched the slight deformity of his harelip with a fingertip, as he often did, rubbing it gently. He bobbed his head a third time. "I won't. I promise. What about your folks? They know?"

Caleb's mouthcorners turned down. "I've tried to tell them. They don't believe me. Think I'm making it up. It happens all the time — the secret thing, I mean — but I'm not going to tell them about it anymore. I'm not going to tell anyone but you."

"Okay, what is it?"

"Promise you won't tell?"

"Jeeze!" Mike exploded, fairly squirming with combined excitement and agitation. "I told you I wouldn't tell, didn't I? I promise, I promise, okay?"

"Okay. Like I said, you probably won't believe it either when I start, but by the time I finish you will. You'll see. Mike, listen," his voice lowered considerably, "I know how to get inside the heads of animals. Inside plants, too."

"Huh?" Mike's mouth had dropped open and his forehead was furrowed. It was obvious he was not comprehending what Caleb was saying.

"I know it's hard to understand, but it's true." Caleb went on without pause, the words coming faster now that the floodgates had been opened. "I can get inside their heads and see everything they're doing, right out of their own eyes. I can hear what they hear and feel everything they feel. I can even smell what they smell and when they eat something, I can taste it, too."

Mike snorted. "Nobody can do anything like that."

"I *can,* honest! I do it all the time. I've always done it. For a long time I thought everybody could do it, just like me, and then I began to find out I'm the only one who can. Go ahead, shake your head, but at least listen to what I'm going to tell you. Remember, I said you wouldn't believe me at first."

For upwards of two hours they lay facing one another, the board game untouched between them, as Caleb went into greater detail about his ability. Gradually young Marlett's skepticism diminished and all but disappeared. He became fascinated and at one point interrupted Caleb's monologue.

"Can you get inside people like that, too?"

Caleb nodded and grimaced. "I don't like to, though. I did it once in a while when I was a little kid, but it sort of scared me. I didn't like the way they felt inside. Most of the time it was pretty ugly. Sometimes," he repeated, "they *really* scared me. I stopped doing it with people at all and now I only go into animals. Sometimes plants. Animals are more fun, though. They do neat things."

He went on to relate in close detail many of his experiences, concluding with the moth and owl experiences of last night and the one with the oak tree this morning. All the while Mike lay there spellbound, no further trace of doubt in his manner.

"Boy!" Mike breathed at last. "Are you ever lucky! Wish I could do it."

"Me, too, but at least now I can tell you about the things that happen when I get into something."

"Yeah, that'll be great." A thought struck Mike and he

looked at Caleb sharply. "Hey, now I know why you sometimes get that blank look on your face and it's hard to get through to you. That's when you're inside some animal, isn't it?"

"Uh huh. Remember yesterday when you came up to me in the park across the street and had to shake my arm?" There was a distant sound of the telephone ringing, but Caleb paid no attention to it. "I was in a redwinged blackbird out in the marsh. I got inside him in the park where I was standing when you found me, but then he flew out into the marsh with the others. I told you I was listening to a bird singing and you couldn't hear it? Well, I was. It was the bird I was in, but he was way out in —"

"Boys!" It was Caleb's mother calling from the foot of the stairs. "Better come on down. Mike, that was your mother who just called. She wants you to come home right away. Your dinner's nearly ready. We'll be eating soon, too, Caleb."

The two boys scrambled to their feet, leaving the unused game spread out on the floor, and thundered down the stairs. They raced outside to where Mike's bicycle was parked. As his friend mounted and prepared to pedal home, Caleb gripped the handlebar and momentarily stayed him. He felt exultant that Mike believed what he said and that at last he could really open up to someone. Talking about his experiences had meant a great deal to him.

"Mike, thanks for believing me."

The red-head shrugged. "No big deal," he said. "Nobody could just make up stuff like you told me. It had to be true. Well, I gotta get going. Want me to come by in the morning?"

"Sure."

"Okay, I'll see you then." He raised a hand in parting and started pumping toward his own house about three blocks away, near the corner of Elim Avenue and Shiloh Boulevard.

Caleb cupped his mouth and shouted after him: "Don't forget the promise you made upstairs, Mike."

"Okay, I won't," came the diminishing voice. "See you in the morning." He turned west at the corner of Shiloh and was out of sight.

Chapter 5

CALEB AND MIKE ARRIVED at East School and parked their bicycles in the well-filled bike rack just as the first bell rang. They jostled along with the other students heading for their various classrooms. The two were in their respective seats a couple of rows apart when the second bell rang and Arlene Olstrohm, seated behind her desk, brought the class to order and called roll.

Miss Olstrohm was tall, a large-boned, angular woman in her middle thirties, her Swedish heritage evident in high cheekbones and square jawline, as well as in the straw-colored hair braided in a circle atop her head. Her watery-blue eyes were warm, although Caleb and the others were well aware that they could quickly turn into chips of glacial ice when she became annoyed. Hers was a well-deserved reputation for making pupils toe the line in accordance with her standards of comportment and learning.

The first period of study was devoted to mathematics.

There was nothing distinctive about it; Miss Olstrohm spent most of the time, after collecting their homework papers, at the blackboard going over new problems with the class. When the hour was completed, she instructed them to put away their math materials. She returned to her desk and leaned against it, facing the class, waiting for the shuffling to die away. Then she straightened.

"For our science period," she announced, "we're going to concentrate on the project I've mentioned to you several times during the past week or so. It deals with both the animal world and the plant world and how they interact. You've learned that in one way or another, most animals depend upon plants for survival, even those animals we call carnivorous. Now, who can tell me what we mean by carnivorous?" Her eyes flicked across the room and stopped on a thin boy with dark curly hair. "Bradley?"

The boy sighed, stood up by his desk, shifted self-consciously for a moment and then took a stab at it. "It means . . ." He paused, cleared his throat, licked his lips and began again, his voice very reedy. "Carnivorous means an animal that catches and eats another animal."

"Not quite," said the teacher. "You've described what we call a predator. You may sit down, and I suggest you pay closer attention to what we're studying. Now, who can give me a more accurate description of what we mean by carnivorous?"

Several hands went up, Caleb's among them, and she called upon him. He stood and said, "Carnivorous means meat-eating."

"That is correct. What, then, do we call an animal that eats only vegetation?"

"Herbivorous."

"And those which eat both flesh and vegetation?"

"Omnivorous."

"Very good, Caleb. You may be seated. Class, those are important words to know and I want you to remember them. They may appear in your final exams.

"Now," she continued, "as we were discussing earlier, flesh-eating animals — carnivores — depend upon plants because, while they do not eat the plants themselves, they eat the animals which eat the plants. This is part of the cycle of life in nature — what we call the food chain. Once in a while, however, nature plays a little trick and turns things around. An example of this is the plant we have over here."

She strode to a wheeled cart by the window, upon which was a terrarium. With her hand on the glass cover, she continued: "Inside here we have a carnivorous plant. It actually, in a manner of speaking, eats flesh; not as you and I do, by chewing and swallowing, but in an entirely different way. This plant grows in marshy ground in some areas of North Carolina and is called a Venus flytrap."

Projecting from the rich black earth in the bottom of the rectangular terrarium was a single bright green plant with several pairs of peculiar, hinged, pod-shaped round leaves. These were lying open on the soil, each pair forming a sort of flat rosette. Along their outer fringes were regularly spaced needle-like spines. There was nothing else inside the rectangular glass enclosure.

Miss Olstrohm wheeled the cart past the front of the room and down the center aisle between the desks, stopping at about the mid-point of the room and only a few feet away from where Caleb sat. The teacher straightened and looked toward the rear of the room.

"Through the efforts of Philip Tompson over the weekend," she told the class, "we will perhaps be able to witness a remarkable thing. Philip?"

A good-looking boy arose from his desk near the back wall and approached her. He was carrying a slender cylindrical jar, which he handed to the teacher. He returned to his seat as she held it aloft for all to see. Inside, crawling aimlessly on the glass lid, were three houseflies. Miss Olstrohm set the jar atop the terrarium glass and looked around.

"I've moved the terrarium here to the center of the room," she explained, "to try to give everyone the best view possible. Those of you who are seated nearby may remain as you are. Those farther away should crowd around as close as possible without obstructing the views of others."

There was a general scuffling and scraping and the murmur of voices as the students moved in. Caleb, still seated, found himself surrounded by others. His eyes were on the trio of flies in the narrow jar and even before Miss Olstrohm had stilled the talking, he had transferred his consciousness into one of the flies.

The air inside the jar was stagnant and very warm. The fly into which Caleb had projected himself moved constantly, seeking escape, crawling around the inside of the glass prison, traversing the length of the jar from its base to the securely screwed-on lid. No air holes had been punched in it. Occasionally the fly bumped into — or was bumped by — one of the other imprisoned flies and then he would feel his fly's wings buzz in a futile attempt at flight within the close confines. The male fly in which Caleb found himself had appeared to him, from a distance, to have a generally black body. Up close, looking through the eyes of the fly at the other two of the same species, he could see this was not entirely accurate. Actually, the color was gray-black on the abdomen and somewhat lighter on the thorax. The thorax itself was striped with four black lines close together, running from front to rear. Over both thorax and abdomen grew a sparse forest of stiff hairs, some black, some gray. Each fly had only two wings, unlike most flying insects which have four, and the pair of wings were glassy clear, interwoven with a network of support veins which helped keep the fragile fabric from tearing when the wings whipped through the air at the incredible speed of hundreds of beats per second.

Still viewing the other two from the fly he inhabited, Caleb could see that the head of each was composed almost entirely of two large reddish-brown compound eyes and a tubular sucking mouthpart. The six legs sprouted stiff hairs and each foot terminated in two claws so minute they could cling with ease to microscopic imperfections on the seemingly smooth glass.

Within his fly, Caleb realized that something had momentarily covered the light. In the dimness he felt movement, a scraping vibration and more movement, ending in a jolt. It became light again and with the light came a rush of fresher air. Instantly Caleb felt his fly turn toward the source. The other two flies exhibited similar reactions. He felt his own male insect's wings buzzing frantically and experienced an exhilarating sense of freedom as he shot from the mouth of the small container. There was soil beneath, and a plant quickly passed by; then his fly slammed into an impenetrable clear wall.

Caleb understood then that the olive jar had been opened and placed on its side on the soil inside the terrarium. He shared the efforts of his fly as he buzzed back and forth, striking the clear walls time and again, much more free to move than before, but still a prisoner. He flew to the upper glass and bumped against it a number of times, then alighted upon it and clung there upside down, resting. A moment later he flew down to the soil, circled briefly and landed.

Bracing himself on his four hind legs, the fly began cleansing himself. Caleb watched as the front legs lifted and came together before the compound eyes, and he felt them rubbing vigorously against one another. One at a time the sucking mouthpart ran over them, cleansing particles of debris from the tiny hairs. Caleb could feel a slight coolness resulting from the infinitesimal moistening of the legs. Then the front legs were rubbed back and forth across the eyes to cleanse the facets, the head turning from side to side as this was being accomplished.

One of the forelegs reached back and hooked around a wing, forcing it forward and upward, cleansing the underside. The wing on the other side was brought up in the same way by the other foreleg and cleaned. The wings were released and the short, barely frilled antennae were scrubbed. After that, Caleb felt the weight of the fly settle to the four front legs as now the hind pair stretched back and rubbed together briefly before reaching forward and rubbing across the upper surfaces of the wings, cleansing them.

While this was occurring, Caleb became aware of a pungent, rather sweetish aroma assailing the fly's olfactory nerves. It originated close by and he shared the fly's walk to the source of the smell, over soil whose surface was like boulders beneath his feet. The appealing scent was emanating from one of the pairs of rosetted spine-fringed leaves open before him, the sharply tapering spikes pointing innocuously upward. Caleb knew it was the Venus flytrap open and waiting, enticing with an irresistible aroma; knew the fly he was inhabiting might become the victim; knew a sense of horror at the fly's inability to comprehend a danger here. Though he knew with certainty from past experience that there was no way he could control the insect's movements, his mind fairly screamed with unuttered warning and he strove to move the fly away through his willpower. As always, it was to no avail; his presence, his own fear, his efforts to control were wholly unsuspected by the host.

The fly stepped over the row of vertical spines and up onto the basin-like pan of one side of the hinged leaf, moving toward the stem area where the scent was strongest. He paid no attention to three little projecting hairs sticking upright in a triangular formation a quarter-inch apart in the center of the leaf. The body of the fly touched one of these hairs and nothing happened. He moved more completely into the trap and barely brushed against a second hair. The two trigger hairs touched in succession were the stimulus the plant required.

With shocking speed the hinged leaf halves snapped together, the hard sharp spines partially meshed like stiff interlocking fingers. By the time the fly could react — and his reaction time was very swift — it was already too late. Caleb felt the wings try to open and fail, because of the pressure against them; felt the legs try to grip and pull and ultimately fail for the same reason. The fly was securely pinned. Through his host's eyes Caleb could see the precise interlocking of the leaf spines and it was as if he peered from behind the bars of a jail cell. But this prison offered much less possibility of escape.

Gradually, very gradually, the pressure grew stronger and the openings between the spines diminished as their thicker bases moved toward one another. The prison cell had become a death chamber and Caleb felt the body of the fly being inexorably crushed. Movement was now so restricted that only one of the fly's six legs could move a little. Soon, even that motion was prevented. The fly's senses were dulling, fading as death approached, but not before Caleb was able to share the fly's pain as a fluid which had been exuding from the inner surface of the leaves saturated the fly's body and began to eat into the tissues; juices so powerful that the chitin and softer flesh quickly began disintegrating.

There was only a bare degree of awareness remaining in the fly when Caleb transferred his consciousness into the Venus flytrap. At once he could feel the powerful fibers of the leaves continuing to tighten, straining against the bulk of the fly's body. He sensed the increased flow of digestive juices from the glands on the inside surfaces of the closed leaves and, at the same time, the reabsorption through microscopic pores of digested portions of the fly's flesh, already converted to a liquid form and flowing into the plant's system. He felt the food-rich juices assimilating and merging with the sap that was coursing through vascular tissues, penetrating into the leaf stem, being carried from there into the main stem and down to the root stock, nourishing and revitalizing the plant's whole being.

There came to Caleb the awareness of a different sensation, a stimulus from an outer source. Another of the open-leaf traps was registering the touch of tiny feet crossing the spiny threshold as the second of the trio of flies in the terrarium was lured to its death. There was no movement of the leaf, no movement of the trigger hairs and yet, in some indefinable way, Caleb knew the plant was suddenly poised to snap closed the terrible toothed doors. Just one touch on an individual trigger hair would cause no reaction, but if the same hair were touched a second time, or if one of the other two hairs were touched, the trap would be activated.

It was a second touch which came on the same hair and the leaping of the jaws of the trap toward one another sent a powerful vibration through the whole plant. Rarely, if ever, did the Venus flytrap miss its prey and it did not miss this time. The instant struggles of the entrapped fly shook the plant at first but very quickly ceased as the pressure increased and made movement impossible.

On the verge of leaving the plant of his own volition and returning to his own consciousness, Caleb was a shade too late. He turned his head and stared into the icy eyes of Arlene Olstrohm. Her sharp fingernails were digging into his upper arm as she gripped and shook him with surprising strength, and her voice was no less frigid than her eyes.

"I said snap out of it, Caleb!"

"I'm . . . sorry, Miss Olstrohm. I didn't mean to . . . to . . . I'm sorry."

The teacher released him and it was only with the greatest of willpower that he refrained from reaching up with his other hand to rub his arm. He blinked his eyes rapidly to hold back tears threatening to spill and sat mutely as she launched into a verbal assault upon him, made even more frightening and powerful by its lack of heat and the awful levelness of her tone.

"For this entire school year I have had to endure your periodic disappearances into some void of your own creation," she told him. "I have tried to overlook it, assuming you would eventually cease doing so on your own, but this seems to have been a mistake. We have a classroom of thirty-seven other students and I refuse to exert greater efforts in your behalf than for any of the others. I am not a hired tutor for your private benefit."

There were snickerings from some of the boys and girls who were now back at their own desks and Miss Olstrohm's head jerked around, silencing them. "I see no cause for levity in this incident," she told them. "The next person who makes a sound will be sent to the office of the principal. Is that understood?"

No one said a word and the teacher returned her attention to Caleb. "The science project today," she went on, "was a very important one, Caleb. I had thought, with your obvious interest in nature, that it was one you would find most absorbing. It appears you could not have cared less about it and, insofar as you are concerned, the entire experiment has been wasted. Your inattention has been disruptive to the class in general, not only today but at frequent intervals in the past. I would not care to have you in my class for another year, but don't think for an instant I will shrink from giving you a failing grade for the year if there is one more example of this inattention of yours before school ends on Friday. The fact that your grades have been better than average has no bearing in the matter whatsoever. Do you understand me?"

"Yes, ma'am." Caleb's cheeks were burning and his hands were clenched so tightly in his lap that they ached.

Miss Olstrohm marched to her desk, her back rigid and head held high, then turned to face the class. There was still not a sound in the room. She looked back and forth across them for a long moment and then nodded as if coming to a decision.

"You all know," she said quietly, "that final exams are scheduled for Wednesday and Thursday. I think I should remind you that all of your classroom work during this final week is, in essence, part of that testing. Since our next period is English I want each and every one of you — including you, Mr. Erikson — to take out writing materials and compose an essay of no less than five hundred words, describing to the best of your ability today's science project concerning the Venus flytrap. Your final grade will reflect the quality — or lack of it! — of what you have written. You may begin."

There were some muffled groans and it was apparent that Caleb's classmates considered him responsible for this assignment. There was little friendship in the looks sent his way as they opened their desks to remove pads and pencils.

The remainder of the morning was one of the quietest

that the East School seventh grade classroom had ever known. There were whispered scratchings of pencils across paper and occasional sighs from those who had rarely written more than a page and a half about anything in their lives before; but mostly there was silence. Miss Olstrohm sat at her desk in front, absorbed in grading their homework papers, until exactly thirty seconds before the noon bell rang, when she looked up and addressed them.

"You may stop writing for the time being. Leave your papers on your desks and be prepared to complete them this afternoon when you return from lunch."

More hard looks were sent in Caleb's direction during the remaining seconds before the bell rang and at least half the class heard the hissed words of Karen Morrison, who sat near him, when she cupped her mouth with one hand and whispered savagely, "You stink, Caleb Erikson!"

Though he did not turn to look at her, he felt a flush creep up his neck and settle in his cheeks and ears. It was still there when the bell sounded. The room emptied in a matter of seconds, but in that short interval of crowding at the door, Caleb was shoved roughly several times and someone he didn't see punched him painfully in the center of the back and he almost fell.

Caleb moved quickly outside to the bike rack and began pedaling home for lunch. A chorus of harsh remarks were hurled at him before he pulled away. The only words of a friendly nature came from Mike Marlett who called out: "Don't worry, Cay, it wasn't your fault." The words were small comfort and dejection was heavy within him when he arrived home.

Deciding he would say nothing to his mother about what had happened, he sat solemnly in the kitchen nook while she prepared a bowl of soup and a hamburger for him. She chatted pleasantly as she worked, making light of a series of minor misfortunes that had plagued her this morning. In addition to painfully breaking one of her fingernails just after Caleb left, she had also pulled a disastrous run in a brand new set of pantyhose and bumped her head sharply on a cupboard door she had left open. To top it off, when she was returning home from the supermarket the final bag of groceries carried into the house had given way and everything tumbled onto the ceramic brick tiles of the kitchen floor. A carton of fresh eggs, a jar of mayonnaise and a quart bottle of very expensive pure maple syrup had collided and all had smashed. It had taken her about an hour to clean up the viscous mess studded with broken glass, and she had cut a finger in the process.

"Just hasn't been my day," she chuckled, setting the soup and hamburger before Caleb and then sitting down across from him with a small serving of soup for herself. Not until then did the realization strike her that Caleb was abnormally quiet and seemed downcast. She was immediately concerned that he was ill and reached over to place a palm on his brow.

"I'm not sick," he told her, pulling away slightly.

Iris withdrew her hand, frowning at the rebuff. "Well, there's obviously *something* bothering you. What's the matter?"

Despite his resolution to say nothing, Caleb abruptly found himself — without mentioning his transference into the fly and Venus flytrap — telling her how Miss

Olstrohm had bawled him out for not paying attention to the classroom science project and had wound up assigning the whole class the writing of an essay during the English period, and that his classmates blamed him for the assignment. He fully expected her to soothe him, as she usually did on those rare occasions when he was troubled, but he had chosen a bad time. Though she had attempted to pass lightly over her own series of mishaps this day, she was still irked about them and her reaction to Caleb's recital was hardly sympathetic.

"In other words, despite our discussion at the dinner table Saturday, you were day-dreaming again, weren't you?"

"No, I wasn't *day-dreaming*."

His emphasis on the final words caused her to purse her lips. "I get the impression we're splitting hairs about words," she told him. "Are you telling me that you weren't making believe again that you were inside some animal? What was it this time — a bird outside the window?"

The boy shook his head violently. "It wasn't *make-believe*, either!" he blurted. "I really got inside the fly, and then inside the plant. I could feel what they —"

"Stop it!" Iris smacked the bowl of her soup spoon against the table with a sharp rap and glared at him. "I don't want to hear it, Caleb. You can't go through life pretending like this. What is the matter with you, anyway? Your father and I are fed up with it. You're getting to be a big boy now and you've got to start acting your age. Now, eat your lunch and then get back to school and don't you dare let yourself go off into your make-believe world anymore or you'll have to answer to your father. I am finished making excuses for you. Now eat!"

Stomach churning, Caleb shook his head. "I'm not hungry."

"Fine! That's just fine! Now what am I supposed to do with this food? Go on, then, get out of here. I don't even want you around when you act like this. And you be sure to come right home after school. Your father wants you to mow the lawn."

Caleb stumbled from the house and aimed his bicycle back toward school. A block from home he stopped and watched two fox squirrels race across the street, one in hot pursuit of the other. At any other time he would have projected himself into one of them, or successively into both. This time he merely stared morosely at them. Dejection was heavier than ever in him and he felt very alone and sorry for himself, convinced at last that even his own parents didn't love him anymore and the only friend he had in the whole world was Mike. With that thought he got back on his bike and headed for Mike's house.

Mrs. Marlett came to the door when he knocked and shook her head when she saw him. "Oh, Caleb, you just missed Michael by a few minutes. For some reason he was in a big hurry today. Gulped down his milk and sandwich like he was starving and then ran right out. He said he had something to do at school, so I'm sure you'll find him there."

Caleb thanked her and left. In no hurry to return to the schoolyard, he pedaled slowly, circled one entire block needlessly and paused briefly to feel sorry for the remains of a dead baby bird on the street. Naked and pink-skinned, with bluish membranes over the unopened eyes, the hatchling had evidently fallen out of a nest in the trees overhead. He looked up, searching the branches, but saw no sign of the nest.

As he arrived at the school and pushed the front wheel of his bike into the rack, he saw Mike with a number of the other boys from his class at one corner of the building. He wanted very much to see Mike, but not the other boys. But the matter was taken out of his hands as they all came toward him in a group. Their first verbal taunts as they neared were devastating.

"Hey, Caleb," Freddie Gardner yelled, "why don't you put your brain inside a gorilla!"

"A rat would be better," chimed in Jeff Hackman. "More his style."

"Go put your brain in a snake," suggested another voice from the rear of the ring of boys now surrounding him, "and crawl into a hole where you belong."

"That's if he's got a brain," someone else piped up.

"Why don't you turn into an owl for us," taunted a brassy voice behind him, "like you did Saturday night."

Paling, Caleb snapped his head around toward the voice and saw that the speaker was Harvey Howe, an obnoxious, loud-mouthed boy he had never liked. Mike Marlett had never liked him either, yet if Harvey knew about what happened with the screech owl, it could only be because Mike had told him. The sudden realization that Mike had betrayed him, had broken his solemn promise not to tell anyone, caused a blinding wave of fury to sweep through him. His eyes were seeking out faces in the crowd and then he saw the red-headed boy hanging back at the outer fringe of the circle. When their eyes met, Mike shook his head and made a helpless gesture.

With a harsh, inarticulate cry, Caleb plunged into the group, shoving boys aside. He was shoved himself and struck several times, but paid no attention. He flung himself upon Mike and together they fell and rolled on the ground in a tangle of arms and legs. A loud chorus of yells erupted and the magnetic cries of "Fight! Fight!" had their effect. In moments the majority of students in the area were converging on them.

Actually, Mike was not fighting, merely trying to defend himself from Caleb's wrath and desperately trying to talk, but Caleb gave him no opportunity. When they stopped rolling over, Caleb was on top with Mike pinned beneath him. Their faces were only inches apart and Caleb was saying over and over, "You told them, Mike, you told them!" His voice was a sobbing rasp. He drew back his fist but before the blow could fall he was grabbed around the neck by Harvey Howe and dragged off backward. The Hackman boy leaped on him, then others, and now the blows were falling in earnest, with Caleb the principal recipient.

It was the heavy-set Wilbur England, eighth grade teacher, who waded through the crowd with elephantine ease, sweeping the massed boys away from in front of him as if they were dominoes and finally separating the chief combatants, Jeff Hackman and Caleb Erikson.

"As I see it," he said mildly, holding each of the boys by the scruff, "either I can knock your heads together or I can take you to the principal's office . . ." — the one o'clock bell rang just then — ". . . or I can let you walk back to your class right now, as if all this never happened. What's it going to be?"

Both boys were panting and showing a few aftereffects of the melee. Caleb was licking a slightly cut lip which had been jammed against a tooth, while Jeff had a swelling beginning to form at the corner of his left eye. Neither boy said anything. Around them the crowd was dispersing as students hurried to their classes.

"Am I to take it you'd prefer the latter?" Mr. England asked quietly.

They nodded and he released them, smiled pleasantly and walked away. Jeff and Caleb looked at one another for a moment and then separated without saying anything, walking toward the main entrance. Mike Marlett moved on an interception course from one side and fell in next to Caleb, who scowled accusingly.

"I trusted you, Mike."

"I'm sorry, Cay, honest. Listen to me. I got back here fast because I heard the guys were going to knock you around for making us get that writing assignment from Miss Olstrohm. I wanted them to know it wasn't your fault." When his friend continued walking without looking at him, Mike's voice took on a pleading quality. "Caleb, listen to me! Don't you see I only told them because I'm proud of you? No one else can do what you do. When we were in class, I knew you'd gone into that fly. I just *knew* it! And when Miss Olstrohm bawled you out, I wanted to stand up and tell her you knew what happened with the fly and the plant better than anyone else in the room. In the whole world, even!"

Caleb stopped and looked at Mike and shook his head,

holding back tears with an effort. "You promised me you wouldn't tell anyone," he said bitterly, "and then you did it anyway. I'll never tell you a secret again. You're no friend. You're a traitor, that's what!"

He walked away, resolute in his determination never again to tell anyone about his special talent, never again to open himself to ridicule. A moment later he entered Miss Olstrohm's classroom, the crestfallen Mike following a few steps behind. The second bell rang just as they took their seats. The teacher moved from her desk to stand in front of the class.

"You may continue your essays in a moment," she told them. Her eyes stopped momentarily on Caleb and then moved on, pausing briefly on others. "I understand there was something of an altercation outside and I want you to know, all of you, that I do not approve. I can understand, considering what has happened, that some of you may feel that it was due to the actions of one person present here that you were given this writing assignment today. I assure you, it was not. You would have received the assignment in any event, but as homework rather than classroom work. I think you would have appreciated that even less." There was a pleased murmuring which ceased as she continued speaking. "I suspect some of you may have been dawdling over your papers and you may now become sorry about that. Your essays must be finished before you leave today. However, as soon as you are finished, bring your work up to the desk and then you are free to leave."

The pleasure turned to outright jubilation and it was several moments before the commotion died down. Miss

Olstrohm returned to her desk but before sitting down she spoke a final time. "This does not give you leave to do hurried, sloppy or careless work," she warned. "Now you may resume your writing."

The class got busy immediately and once again silence prevailed in the room. Miss Olstrohm continued grading their homework papers as they worked and an hour passed. Most of the students were having a certain amount of difficulty composing an essay of five hundred words about something that many of them had considered more or less inconsequential while they were observing it. Caleb had no such difficulty. His pencil flew across the paper and only occasionally did he pause, considering. A few minutes after two o'clock he walked to the front of the room and placed the eight sheets of handwriting that made up his essay on Miss Olstrohm's desk.

The teacher looked up and the corners of her mouth twitched in the trace of a smile. "I hardly expected anyone would be finished this quickly, Caleb. Especially you. I said you could leave when you were finished, but do you mind waiting here a moment while I glance at what you've written?"

"No ma'am." His stomach tightened.

He watched as she read. Twice she corrected his spelling with her red ballpoint pen and at one place she wrote the words "improper tense" in the margin and circled it, indicating a particular sentence. She finished it quickly with no other marks, picked up the papers and tapped them on the desk to align them neatly, then set the small stack before her again. She still hadn't looked up. Once more she picked up the red pen and this time wrote three words across the top of the first page: *"Anthropomorphic, but excellent!"*

The teacher looked up at Caleb and her smile was genuine, her voice soft, hardly above a whisper. "It appears I may have been hasty in my assumption that you were not paying attention this morning, Caleb." She wrote a large letter A at the upper right-hand corner and circled it. "You're free to go now," she said.

"Thank you, Miss Olstrohm." He left the room but did not immediately go outside. Instead, he followed the hallway to the school library and went in. The large room with its numerous tiers of shelves filled with books was very familiar to him and he walked immediately to where there was a large unabridged *Webster's Dictionary* resting on a stand of its own. Though he was pleased at his teacher's words and the grade she had given his paper, he did not know the meaning of the word "anthropomorphic" and wanted to look it up before he forgot how to spell it. He turned the large thin pages carefully and found the entry without difficulty. He read it slowly:

Described or conceived in a human form or with human attributes; represented with human characteristics or under a human form; ascribing human characteristics to non-human things.

He was smiling as he left the library, but the expression faded by the time he reached his bicycle. As he pedaled north on Elim Avenue, he was not happy. Miss Olstrohm's final words had cheered him somewhat and he was not particularly bothered by the fact that she thought his essay was anthropomorphic, but everything else seemed terrible: His parents didn't seem to like him very much, and his best friend had violated a trust, broadcasting his secret after having promised not to do so. Nothing seemed right anymore. There was no one to whom he could turn, no one to whom he could talk. He felt unloved, unwanted, betrayed and, most of all, unneeded. His only solace seemed to lie in nature, where everything was simple and straightforward. He wished desperately that he could just merge permanently with the animal world and never have to bother with people again.

By this time he had reached Shiloh Boulevard and he turned east and picked up speed, heading for the Lake Michigan shore. He knew there were things he should do, but he didn't care. The lawn had to be mowed, for one thing, but his mother didn't expect him home from school for at least another hour, so that could wait. He also realized he should see to his garden and replant the areas where the rabbit had eaten the sprouts, but that could be done later. Mike usually came over after school, but Caleb had no desire to see him, no longer wished to share with him the joy and peace and fascination he found in nature. Caleb Erikson was no longer willing to let himself become vulnerable.

Near the shore of the lake he turned north on an abandoned tarmac road that had been blocked to motor vehicles by sawhorse barricades. As he pedaled slowly along the deserted road he saw, not far ahead, a bird with thin legs and a light-colored body. It took off on long narrow wings and flew toward him, just above the pavement, for a hundred feet or so. When it landed, only forty or fifty feet away, Caleb saw the flash of a conspicuous rusty spot of plumage at the base of the tail, from which he correctly identified the bird as a killdeer. It had landed on the road again and was standing still, looking at him, its short pointed tail bobbing nervously. Although it was a bird he had occasionally seen before, Caleb had never entered one and now he succumbed to the temptation of *in*-sight. He stopped and pushed the kick-stand of the bike into place and then turned and looked at the bird, simultaneously entering it.

As always, it was with a slight start and sense of amusement that he viewed himself with the bird's vision, standing beside the bike. When the boy didn't move, the bird dipped its head and ran rapidly on its long narrow legs for a dozen feet, stopping on the shoulder of the road and looking again. The boy had not moved, but now Caleb felt the wings outstretch and he was aloft, flying with dizzying speed close to the ground. He felt the jaw muscles stretch as the beak opened wide and the throat muscles swelled. The high-pitched *B-deee! B-deee! B-deee!* rolled out and filled the bird's aural cavities. To Caleb, it was one of the most delightful sounds he had ever heard.

The bird, a male, angled up in a steep climb. A hundred feet or more above the ground he leveled off and flew with rapid wingbeats toward the lake. The wind rushing past picked up intensity and the bird wheeled erratically, set his wings and swept downward at such a steep angle that Caleb, viewing the ground rushing up to meet him, was sure a crash was inevitable. Mere inches above the beach the killdeer leveled off, flying northward. He skimmed just above the margin of sand and water, veered sharply to the left and sped over the bank out into the area of coarse grasses that rose from the sandy soil in brushlike tufts. The bird's vision was remarkably keen and its gaze touched upon a small dark beetle lumbering across an opening on the ground.

The veering before had been nothing compared to what happened now. Wings and tail flared in unison and the bird spun into an incredibly tight turn at high speed, his breast plumage all but touching the tips of the grasses. There occurred another flaring of the wings and tail, a braking action and a drop to the ground, with the stilt-like legs instantly striding out and matching the landing speed of the bird. A dozen running paces and he was back to the proper clearing and snatched up the beetle in his beak just as the insect was reaching cover.

For a moment Caleb contemplated entering the beetle, but then decided against it and stayed inside the killdeer. Sticking out on either side of the beak he could see the legs and a part of the shiny black upper wing cases of the beetle protruding. The killdeer took off again and flew in a direct line toward a graveled area close to the same road the boy was on, but a mile north of him.

Caleb felt the throat swell as a garbled version of the bird's song emerged while he landed more delicately on the fringe of the gravel. Though Caleb was sure there was no place for anything to hide on the open surface of the small stones, four little figures that had been crouched in perfect mimicry of the rocks suddenly stood up high and ran toward him. Fuzzy and tiny, with legs like long pinkish toothpicks, the baby killdeers clustered near the parent bird, outstretching ridiculous little down-covered wings and peeping plaintively. Their bodies looked like miniature dirt-stained tennis balls. Bright black eyes glittered in anticipation and they were obviously very hungry.

Caleb's host bird clenched his beak and shook his head, biting the beetle into fragments and scattering them on the stones. There were two large pieces and one smaller and, though they fell among the crevices of the rocks, no piece was wasted. In a second all had been consumed and the infants that had eaten them cried for more, but not quite so stridently as the one who had eaten nothing.

The male's head cocked and Caleb could see the female coming in, her own beak gripping a bright green katydid. As the male had done, she landed, then bit and shook her prey, flinging the pieces away for the baby birds to eat. The chick that had missed a piece before snatched up and devoured the largest portion this time. One final piece remained in the female's mouth and she stuffed it in the open maw of the nearest of her young, who was begging piteously.

The male and female, similarly colored, stepped toward one another and touched beaks momentarily. Then the female made a low sound. At once the four baby birds ran in different directions for several feet, stopped and squatted among the stones, burying their heads in their breast fuzz. In that split second they had so miraculously camouflaged themselves that, had not he seen them do it, Caleb would have been unable to find them.

Both adults took off at the same time and separated.

Once more Caleb joined in the exhilarating process of ranging back and forth close above the grasses. Another insect was caught — a grasshopper — and again there was the flight back to the gravel area and the feeding of the young. This time the female was not there; but the next time his host came back, again with a grasshopper, she was already there feeding them.

Caleb transferred to her and discovered there was little difference between them. She was perhaps a shade smaller than the male and, if anything, even a little more agile in flight. The exultation of participating in such aerial maneuverings and the delight of seeing the baby killdeers feed kept Caleb with the bird for trip after trip as she and her mate attempted to sate the insatiable appetites.

Then, with a horrified sensation, he saw through the female's eyes that the sun was low in the west. Just as she was taking wing again, he transferred back into his own body. The exhilaration was gone, replaced by a heavy concern for what he would now have to face at home. He couldn't believe he had stayed out so long. His promise to come home and mow the lawn after school was broken. His father certainly was home from work by now and it was already well past dinner time. Though he stood up on the pedals and pumped as fast as he could, there was no way to make up the lost time.

Once again Caleb had gotten himself into trouble.

Chapter 6

DESPITE THE FACT that Caleb was promoted to the eighth grade on Friday, the final days of this week had not been a happy time for him. The atmosphere at home had been decidedly chilly. Following an initially severe reprimand for coming home late on Monday, not mowing the lawn as instructed, missing dinner and worrying his parents considerably, he had been grounded for the remainder of the week and assigned a series of small jobs that kept him busy. Since Warren and Iris would be leaving on their trip early Monday, the plan was to take Caleb to Algonquin on Sunday to begin his summer-long stay at Spring Hill Farm.

Caleb had never felt so alone. Not only hadn't Mike called or come over all week, he had also successfully avoided Caleb in school. Worse yet, there had been no opportunity to enter the consciousness of any animals. Thus, when Friday arrived and all his classmates were jubilant at being promoted and having a long summer vacation at hand, he did not share their happiness.

Now it was Saturday and Caleb had spent the morning on his hands and knees in his garden, pulling out the new weeds that had sprouted and carefully planting fresh seeds where the rabbit had eaten the sprouts a week ago. He realized it was probably a wasted effort now; the whole garden was, since he would not be here to tend it. The thought compounded his melancholy.

With the work finished, he put away his tools and cleaned up, then joined his parents for lunch, eating mechanically and saying little. Aware of his mood, Warren and Iris attempted to cheer him up by exhibiting enthusiasm about what lay ahead for him.

"I have an idea," his father told him, "that this is going to turn out to be the best summer vacation you've ever had. You're going to be able to see and do things you can't even imagine yet."

Caleb looked at him noncommitally for a long moment and then gave a half-hearted nod. Iris's smile was faintly strained as she took up the theme.

"We talked with Judy Boyle on the phone this morning and she says everything's all set for your arrival tomorrow. We'll drive over in the morning and all have lunch with her. She said she wants to take you through the barn to see the horses and things before your dad and I leave to come back here."

Still Caleb said nothing. Warren reached over and placed his hand on the back of his son's neck with genuine affection. "Look, Caleb, we know it's been a difficult week for you and that you're not happy about our leaving. Believe me, the time will go quickly and we'll all be back together again before you know it. And you really will have a good time at Spring Hill. We'll write you from wherever we are and then, when we get back, you can fill us in on all the things you did at the farm."

"That'll be nice." There was no trace of enthusiasm in his response.

Warren paused and glanced at Iris, then looked back at Caleb. He squeezed his neck gently and withdrew his hand. "Okay, now let's talk about today," he said. "Your mother and I were talking things over while we were packing this morning and we decided that since you've been behaving yourself very well these last few days, we'll lift the restriction. You're free to do whatever you want this afternoon, okay?"

Caleb nodded. "Okay," he said, not caring very much and wishing, as so often in the past, that they could all do something together once in a while. "Is it all right if I go out now?"

"Sure, go ahead. Are you going to use your bike?" At Caleb's nod, he continued. "All right, we'll tie it on the roof of the car in the morning, then, before we leave. In the meanwhile, we'll load up your clothes and the books you wanted and whatever else you might need."

Caleb rose and walked toward the door but stopped and turned as his father spoke to him again.

"You will be home by dinner time, won't you?"

"I'll be home," Caleb promised.

Iris got up from the table and walked to him, hugged him close to her and kissed him on the cheek. Her eyes were overbright as she smiled at him. "We love you very much, you know."

"Sure." He disengaged himself from her and left the

room without looking back, an encompassing loneliness inside, angry at the tears he found filling his eyes. There was relief in the knowledge that his confinement had ended, but it didn't seem to make much difference in his mood. Deep inside he harbored a strong sense of guilt that he couldn't quite understand. He felt that if somehow he had been a better son, more thoughtful and obedient, his parents would not even have considered going on such a long trip without him. Obviously, he had become a disappointment to them, failed to measure up. He yearned to be able to talk with someone about how he felt but there was no one to fill his need. The unfathomable guilt and loneliness that flooded him were all but unbearable.

Walking slowly toward the tool shed where his bicycle was parked, he knew what he was going to do now, but there was something else he had to do first. Mounting his bike, he headed for the house of his red-headed friend. The memory of one thing that Mike had said after their fight had plagued him all week: *"Don't you see? I told them because I'm proud of you."* The shame he felt at having rejected Mike had become a substantial burden.

Mr. Marlett was on his hands and knees in the front yard, using a long-bladed tool forked on the end like a snake's tongue to dig out dandelions. His bald head was speckled with bright beads of perspiration. As Caleb stopped, he looked up and grinned, using a forefinger to shove his rimless glasses back in place.

"How are you, Caleb? Haven't seen you around lately."

"I'm okay, Mr. Marlett. Been sort of busy, I guess. Mike home?"

"Matter of fact, he's not. He and Chuck and Jack took

off somewhere on their bikes a couple of hours ago. I think he said they were going to play ball over at West School. I'm surprised you didn't go along with them. You could probably find them over there if you went."

Caleb shook his head. If Mike had gone alone, he might have sought him out, but not if he were with Chuck and Jack. "No, I don't think I'll do that. I'll see him later, I guess. Would you . . ." He hesitated, then began again. "Mr. Marlett, would you give Mike a message for me when you see him?"

"Certainly."

"Tell him I came over and that I'd like to see him." He paused and then added, "And tell him I'm sorry." He didn't wait for a response, but wheeled his bike around and pedaled east on Shiloh, leaving Mike's father looking after him with a quizzical smile.

Caleb followed Shiloh Boulevard east across the Chicago and Northwestern tracks and coasted down the slight grade to where the wide street arrowed through the expansive marshlands. It was a warm day and the buzzing of insects was a constant musical din among the reeds. A profusion of butterflies whirled about, briefly chasing one another and then breaking away to alight on blossoms here and there. Most of them were the small white cabbage butterflies, but occasionally there were monarchs, fritillaries, painted ladies and dog-faced butterflies, the latter with the black and yellow of their forewings arranged in a delightful silhouette of a dog's profile, complete even to the eye. Caleb paid scant attention to them today.

A gravel road turned off to the left through the marsh

and he followed it for a quarter-mile before turning onto a little foot trail with brush growing so close on both sides that it swished across his arms as he rode through it. After he had penetrated about a hundred yards, it opened up onto a grassy, slightly raised area some fifty feet across, beyond which was a pool of open water in the marsh. A single Carolina poplar, very straight and about a foot in diameter, grew from the raised earth close to the edge of the pond. Many times before, Caleb had come here to sit with his back against the deeply scored bark of the tree and watch the activities of the creatures frequenting the open water on three sides. This was a place he had discovered two years ago and had never shared with anyone, not even Mike; a secret place all his own where he could find isolation from the outside world and its frustrations; a secluded place where he could almost convince himself he was marooned on a desert isle in some uncharted ocean.

The open water was not very extensive. It formed a sort of kidney-shaped pond about twenty feet across and perhaps a hundred feet in a semicircle from one end to the other along its outer perimeter. There were no shore-lines save for that formed by the little island of high ground, the rest being green walls of cattails rising straight up from the water. The pond itself was very clear, its bottom dark with matted vegetation interspersed with soft fern-like water weeds of emerald green.

Caleb leaned his bike against the tree and sat down, cushioned by a short, dense weed cover. He drew his legs up against his chest and locked his arms around them, closing his eyes. The sun was warm on his bare arms and the liquid warblings of redwinged blackbirds touched his ears intermittently, interspersed with occasional soft quackings from a duck deeper in the marsh. The isolated chatter of a passing kingfisher punctuated the air, scolding Caleb for his presence below the tree where the bird had planned to perch over the open water. From a greater distance came the raucous croaking cry of a bittern.

After a few minutes the boy opened his eyes and changed position, stretching out on his stomach with his hands under his chin and elbows jutting outward, his vision directed at a downward angle into the water. Here, where it was very shallow, a tiny crayfish hardly half an inch long was crawling across the bottom. Caleb considered transferring his consciousness into the crustacean, but decided against it when a little silvery minnow, no longer than the crayfish, swam into view. He'd been in crayfish before and found them not terribly interesting, but he had never gone into a minnow.

With the thought he was inside the minute fish, hovering with the tiny pectoral fins barely moving and the gill plates rapidly opening and closing with the motion of the mouth. He felt the surge of water brought in and then, as the mouth closed, felt it being held momentarily against the fleshy red gills. In that fraction of time, oxygen was extracted from the liquid and entered the little fish's system, while simultaneously carbon dioxide was released into the water. Then the gill plates opened and the used water was expelled. Immediately the mouth opened again, drawing in a fresh supply of water. The process was automatic and the fish itself seemed unaware it was occurring, but Caleb was thrilled by it.

The young crayfish just below turned and faced the

minnow, defiantly raising its tiny pincers. It was no real danger, but instantly the minnow jerked its tail and shot away into deeper waters. Its vision was quite good, the eyes set in such a manner that it could see well in most directions. At the slightest movement, the little fish would become alert with muscles tensed to flick away if danger threatened. Approaching the bottom it paused, gaze locked on a strange creature atop a small rock. Caleb studied it closely through the minnow's vision: a dull brown, segmented creature with a peculiar lump on its back. It lay outstretched, wholly motionless, its six legs anchored to the mossy-brown surface of the stone. The huge eyes were the same color as the body and Caleb marveled at how well camouflaged it was. The six legs identified it to him as an insect, but he had no idea what kind.

The minnow acted curious and, since the strange thing was not moving, the fish's initial alarm passed and its muscles relaxed. Neither powerful jaws nor stinger were visible and there was nothing about the creature's appearance that bespoke a possible hazard. The only indication that it was even alive was a barely perceptible pulsing of the gills, far at the rear of its body. Even this movement ceased as curiosity drew the minnow closer. Evidently confident of its ability to flash away at the barest suggestion of peril, the little fish moved to within a half-inch of the creature. That was too close.

With blinding speed a stout, jointed, armlike device shot out from beneath the animal's chest. At its end was a pair of formidable widespread pincers which snapped together on contact with the minnow's belly. Their power was such that they were driven deep into the flesh. Through the minnow's senses, Caleb felt the bloom of acute pain and the instantaneous reactive straining as the tiny fish struggled to get away. There was no way it could break the terrible grip.

It was a fearsome yet exciting experience and Caleb, even though he didn't know what the attacking animal was, transferred himself into it. Now he could see the minnow impaled on the peculiar arm and felt the strong muscles of the creature tighten even more. The pincers sliced through the internal organs of its prey and the struggles of the minnow weakened. A little stream of blood from the fish's stomach drifted off in the water and dissipated. The motions of its gills became faster, much faster, then stopped and the struggling ceased. The minnow was dead.

After a moment more, Caleb saw and felt the jointed arm retracting, drawing the fish's body in close until it was directly beneath the insect's face. Powerful tong-like mandibles bit into the flesh and the creature began eating the morsels rapidly. The meat was oily and rich to the insect's taste, which Caleb shared. The fish was devoured without pause and then the insect used the mandibles to reach down into the container formed under its face by its folded weapon. Bits of flesh that had fallen there were picked up and neatly deposited in the mouth.

Enthralled, Caleb continued to sense and interpret impressions from the strange animal. He knew that it was a female and that her gills were located on the hind end of the digestive system, now so satisfyingly full. He could feel the rhythmic expansion and contraction of her body walls, and knew this movement acted like a pump, forcing water in and out over the gills, which were feathery little masses. Oxygen from the water diffused through the gill surfaces and into the insect's air tubes.

For the first time since his entry into her, Caleb felt the animal beginning to walk. The six legs were long and she crawled with surprising speed across the bottom. At one point she stopped suddenly and through her eyes Caleb detected a large sunfish hoving into view, appearing as a great shadow, slightly above and to one side. The fish was considerably larger than the insect and Caleb was sure his host would be snatched up and eaten. Instead, she expanded her body to its limit, taking in a great volume of water through the gill opening. Then the body walls contracted sharply, expelling the water in a terrific spurt. As if jet propelled, the insect left the bottom and shot away from the sunfish into the darker depths. Twice more while in movement she took in and ejected water, finally settling on the dark bottom at least a dozen feet from where she had started and immediately digging into the debris and hiding herself.

For several minutes she stayed there, unmoving. Caleb, gathering no new sensations, was on the verge of leaving her and returning to his own body when the insect began moving again. Curious — not only about what would happen now, but about what kind of an insect she was — he stayed with her. There was not much visibility here on the bottom, but in a short while something loomed ahead and the insect approached it directly. It turned out to be the base of a cattail reed which she began climbing without hesitation. Even as she neared the surface her pace did not slacken, but she did evacuate, expelling the indigestible residue of the minnow recently eaten. Visibility increased as she continued upward and then, as she emerged from the water, she was momentarily dazzled by the unaccustomed direct sunlight.

The insect continued her climb until she reached a point about a foot above the water's surface. After a momentary pause, she sidled around the cluster of cattail blades until, while still in direct sunlight, she had moved out of sight of the open water and was fairly well hidden from view by the principal bank of cattails growing behind her. Here she sat still, locking her legs tightly on the plant. A light breeze was blowing and the cattail swayed gently with it. In a surprisingly short time the moisture on her body had evaporated. To Caleb, the sensation on the whole body was reminiscent of one he had experienced on his fingertips when he had accidentally smeared them with model airplane cement. The glue had contracted as it dried, crinkling the skin, and that was very much what he felt through the insect's senses now.

With a suddenness that startled him, there was a harsh ripping pop as the skin on the insect's back split from the top of the thorax, just behind the head, all the way down to about the third segment of the abdomen. At once Caleb felt her muscles tighten and she began squirming vigorously, pushing herself backwards and thrusting outward a new soft body from within the old skin.

Caleb had not before experienced metamorphosis, but he knew what it was, having seen movies in school of monarch butterflies emerging from their chrysalides after pupating. This insect he was inhabiting, whatever it was, had been in nymph form when he entered it and now it was shedding its immature skin and emerging as an adult. The sensations were peculiar, though not unpleasant; a sort of combined itching, stretching, expanding.

The abdomen came free first, bent double as it emerged, then springing free and straightening. Wings and back were next and there was no difficulty since the wings were very pliable, having been folded and curled and compressed in the peculiar lump Caleb had first noted on her back as he had viewed her through the minnow's eyes. The head was next to come free, equipped with enormous compound eyes that covered most of her head and even abutted one another at the top. The antennae were notably small — an indication, along with the huge eyes, that this insect depended more upon sight than upon the sense of smell. And at last Caleb was able to identify what it was he was inhabiting: the nymph was metamorphosing into a very large adult dragonfly.

Last to be freed were the legs, at first soft and supple, pulling easily from the sheaths of old skin in which they were bound and very quickly drying into long, slender limbs with a great many sharp bristles on each side. These six legs were set far forward on the thorax. Now she was entirely free and the brown husklike casing of her former self still clung to the reed in the same position in which it had been locked, a mere shell devoid of life.

While the struggle of extrication had been occurring, Caleb had felt fluids from inside her body being pumped into the wings and the resultant unfurling of the wings as they expanded to full length, becoming four distinct long flat planes held horizontally outward from the body. This was the position in which they would always stay, for Caleb knew that this was one of the few winged insects in the world that could not fold its wings. Their span was easily over four inches. Through the insect's eyes, which could see backward as well as forward, sideways and downward, Caleb could see that the surface of the wings was clear, much like cellophane, and very shiny in the sunlight. She was now a beautiful iridescent green dragonfly, the color extending even into the eyes. Her body was long and pointed, like a darning needle. Caleb remembered that when he first encountered dragonflies, he, along with most of his friends, believed the dragonfly carried a fearsome stinger in its long tail, but he later learned this was not true.

Everything Caleb was experiencing about this insect was marvelous. The bulging compound eyes, Caleb knew, comprised twenty-eight thousand microscopic six-sided facets, each facet a system for sight and each equipped with its own tiny lens, a light-transmitting system and highly sensitive retinal cells. Because of the curvature of the eye, not one of those many facets pointed in the same direction as any other. Through each of them Caleb saw a distinct image — a single part of what was being looked at — and the composite form of all these images together resulted in a picture like a mosaic made of twenty-eight thousand tiny tiles. And Caleb knew that, as with all insects with vision, the eyes could neither close nor focus.

The sharpness of the dragonfly's vision was far greater than that of any other insect Caleb had inhabited. He felt a certain smugness about knowing the reason why. From the books he had read in the school library, he was aware that where compound eyes were concerned, the fewer the number of facets, the less perfect the picture. Most insects he'd inhabited had had so few that they saw little more than bulk or movement. Even each eye of the housefly he had entered in the classroom had only two thousand facets, allowing it to see no farther than a few feet at best. Through the eyes of this female dragonfly, however, he could easily see across the pond to the shape of the boy lying on his stomach, looking into the water. And as a further aid to her vision, Caleb now discovered, the dragonfly's head had a hollow at its rear and was loosely attached to the thorax, so that it could swivel and look in different directions.

In the minutes since she had emerged, the dragonfly's body and wings had dried thoroughly, to the point where, when she flapped her wings vigorously in a trial, they rustled and rattled with a tiny clatter. Without further delay she launched herself away from the cattail and flew. Caleb stayed with her, amazed to find that the front and hind wings did not beat in unison, as with other insects. Instead, the hind wings went down as the front wings went up and then vice versa, so rapidly that she could dart or soar or hover with equal ease.

Her emergence as an adult had expended a great deal of energy and Caleb shared her hunger as she flew with great agility some five feet over the pond. He noted that she drew up her long spiny legs beneath her body so that they formed a sort of basket, with its opening toward the front. Her speed increased and she left the pond, skimming rapidly over the marsh in a quest for prey. Her flight path intersected that of a deer fly and, though she was traveling at a speed approaching sixty miles an hour, she spun around in an incredibly sharp turn, followed the deer fly by sight and overtook it.

The deer fly, half again as large as the housefly Caleb had inhabited, was flying in a direct line and did not see the approaching danger until Caleb's dragonfly was only a few feet away. It maneuvered wildly in its attempt to escape, but to no avail. The dragonfly easily countered every move, swept in with blinding speed and neatly scooped the fly out of midair into the basket she had formed with her legs. The momentum caused the fly to become impaled on the spines and though it struggled to get free, it could not.

Still in full flight, the dragonfly bent her head down and Caleb shared the experience as the tong-like mandibles anchored at the sides of her mouth reached into the basket-trap and gripped the fly, forcing it into her maw. There the inner jaw not only gripped the prey but turned it over and over as she ate, as if it were impaled on a spit. In this way, she ate the softer portions of the fly's flesh with ease and discarded such inedible portions as the wings and legs. The food brought new energy to the dragonfly and Caleb felt a sensation of greater strength and ability come to his host. Within a minute or so she had devoured the fly and began her search for new prey.

The whole encounter with the dragonfly — entering its nymph, sharing its metamorphosis and participating in its skillful hunting — had been one of the most absorbing experiences Caleb had ever had in any creature. He was reluctant to leave her, yet he knew it was time he should be heading home. The dragonfly was skimming swiftly over the tops of the cattail reeds when he left her and returned to his own form.

On the island, Caleb sat up and stretched mightily. For the first time in five days the devastating depression that had enshrouded him had lifted and he felt good. He guessed it was not yet even five o'clock, so he certainly wouldn't be late in getting home this evening. Maybe after dinner he'd go over to Mike's house; perhaps even tell him about the dragonfly experience.

In a few minutes he was back on Shiloh Boulevard, whistling in a carefree manner as he pedaled toward home. The thought struck him then that just as the dragonfly had undergone drastic changes in its metamorphosis to adult life, he too would be undergoing a sort of metamorphosis beginning tomorrow. He had the sudden premonition that his would be no less drastic than the dragonfly's.

Chapter 7

WITH THE REAR STORAGE COMPARTMENT of the station wagon well filled and Caleb's bicycle firmly tied to the luggage rack on the roof, Iris and Warren Erikson were ready to leave, but they did not hurry their son.

The boy stood on the front sidewalk, staring at the big old house that had been the only home he'd ever known. For a moment it took on for him the aspect of the dragonfly's larval shell, empty and now to be left behind in lieu of a new life. He knew that was ridiculous — that he'd be gone from it only for the summer — yet the feeling of irrevocable change remained strong in him. It was difficult for him to tear his gaze away from the house, even though he knew his parents were waiting for him. When he heard the slight sound behind him, he thought it was one of them and didn't turn, not until the hand touched his arm.

"Cay?" It was Mike, sad-faced and nervous, his bike parked at the curb behind them. As Caleb faced him he dropped his hand and smiled hesitantly. "I'm sorry I wasn't home when you came over yesterday. My dad said he saw you. Told me what you said."

Caleb nodded. "He said you went over to West School. I was hoping we could've gotten together for my last afternoon here."

"You're really leaving? For the whole summer?" Mike's lower lip quivered as he spoke.

Caleb nodded again. "I'll be staying on a horse farm in Algonquin. That's not so far away." He gestured toward the car. "Only about an hour away."

"Far enough. I wish you weren't going, Cay." He paused, then added: "I'll miss you."

Caleb shrugged, touched, his eyes and throat flooded. "No choice," he said. "I'll miss you, too, Mike. I . . . wanted to tell you — I'm sorry."

Mike shook his head savagely. "No!" he blurted. "I am! It was my fault. I promised I wouldn't tell anybody, then I did. You had a right to be mad."

"Not like that. I shouldn't've jumped you."

They stood quietly, remembering, not knowing what to say, embarrassed, hurting inside. Abruptly Caleb held out his hand and they shook.

"You're still my best friend, Mike."

"And you're mine. I really don't want you to go, Cay."

"I know. I've got to." He made a strange grunt. "No choice."

"Will you write to me?"

"Sure, Mike. You, too?"

"Uh huh."

"Maybe you could come back in about a month and stay with me for a few days. You think so?"

"Maybe, Mike. I don't know."

They weren't saying what they wanted to say, but the words they sought were too elusive and they lapsed into silence. At length Caleb sniffed and walked toward the car, touching Mike's wrist in passing. At the station wagon he opened the back door and then turned around. His friend was rooted where he left him.

" 'Bye, Mike."

" 'Bye, Cay. Luck!"

Caleb got in and shut the door. There was just room enough to sit on the right side of the seat, the rest of the space taken up with hanging clothing, boxes and shoes. On the floor near his feet was his new softball.

"Are you ready to go, Caleb?"

Iris had turned around in her seat and was looking back at him, smiling. She patted his hand, which was resting on the back of her seat. Warren was looking at him in the rearview mirror.

"Yes," he murmured.

Warren put the car in gear and began pulling away. As he did so, Caleb snatched up the softball, leaned out the window and tossed it toward the red-headed boy. It fell short and rolled toward his feet.

"It's yours, Mike," he shouted. " 'Bye!"

They turned out of the driveway onto Edina and Caleb's view was cut off until they reached Shiloh and turned left. As they did so he caught a glimpse of Mike, who was holding the softball against his chest with one hand. The other was lifted in a motionless wave. Then they were out of sight and Caleb realized he hadn't even looked at the house a final time as they were pulling away. He shook his head, murmuring, "It doesn't matter."

"What did you say, dear?" his mother asked.

"Nothing."

They tried for a short while to draw him into conversation, but his answers were monosyllabic and it was obvious he didn't care to talk. They lapsed into silence and Caleb merely stared out the window at the familiar buildings and streets they were passing. The drive to Algonquin, with the traffic somewhat heavier than they expected, took just over an hour. They drove through the small town and then north on Pyott Road. In less than a mile more, Warren pointed to their left.

"This looks like it."

A half-dozen riders were training in a large outside lot adjacent to the road. Beyond them and farther ahead were several large low barns. The nearest of these was faced with a veranda, ordinary doors and windows. A large parking lot was in front of that barn and a curved lane ran from it a hundred yards to the road. Here, on a tall post, there was a white sign with red lettering:

SPRING HILL FARM
RIDING SCHOOL
Boarding – Lessons

"Keep going past," Iris told her husband. "Judy said to come right to her house, about half a mile beyond the barns on the right. We'll be coming back here later on."

"Right," Warren said. "Quite a layout, isn't it, Caleb? Judy told your mother that they have about a hundred horses — their own and boarders — and almost all of them are thoroughbreds."

Prepared to be blasé about it, Caleb was impressed. "It really does look nice," he said, craning his head to see past the clutter of clothes and boxes. It was the most he had spoken at one time since they left Zion.

About a minute later Warren turned into a driveway and they stopped beside a modern brick ranch-type house. He turned around to look at his son, giving him a wink. "Welcome home . . . for the summer. We'll unload the car after a while. Let's go inside first and get acquainted with Judy."

There was a small white entry porch on the front of the house and as they stepped up on it, the front door opened. Judy Boyle welcomed them with obvious pleasure, hugging Iris and kissing her cheek and then shaking hands with Warren and Caleb in turn as Iris introduced them. Judy was a pleasant-looking woman with short dark hair just beginning to gray. Her figure was trim, accented by fitted slacks and a comfortable open-neck shirt. It was her face that caused Caleb to feel attracted to her immediately — open, friendly, marked with faint lines of character that a placid life could not have carved, but which added to her attractiveness. Her light brown eyes were warm as she cocked her head and appraised the boy.

"So you're Caleb, eh? Glad to have you here. Are you a rider?"

Caleb shook his head. "No ma'am. I've never been on a horse."

She lifted an eyebrow. "We'll have to do something about that, won't we? And if you're going to be staying here with me, to you I'm just Judy, not ma'am, okay?" Even as the boy smiled, she turned her gaze to his parents. "Well, don't just stand there. C'mon in. Lunch is all ready. We can bring in Caleb's things when we're finished."

She led them into the living room, at the far end of which was a large fireplace. There were many potted plants in the room, more than Caleb had ever seen in a house, and it reminded him of the time he had visited the Lincoln Park Conservatory in Chicago. They were primarily ferns, philodendrons, pothos and other tropical plants, all of them large and healthy appearing. He could see no sign of wilting. While the adults paused a moment to discuss the room, he swiftly entered the consciousness of half a dozen or more in succession, then returned to himself with his momentary absence not even noted. He walked to one of the plants he had entered and stood looking down at it.

Judy glanced at him and her eyes crinkled. "I gather you like plants, Caleb. I do, too. Horses first, then my plants. What do you think of these?"

"They're nice," he replied, "and in good condition, too, except for this one." He indicated the big split-leaf philodendron at his feet.

The expression on Judy's face became speculative. "Why? What's wrong with it?"

Caleb grinned. "It's not too happy. It doesn't have enough room for its roots."

Warren was frowning and appeared about to speak,

but Judy beat him to it. "Strange you should say that. I very nearly repotted that one this morning. I've been putting it off for weeks." She put her arm around his shoulder. "I have an idea we're going to get along just fine. Well, c'mon, let's eat and get acquainted."

By the time they had finished lunch and carried Caleb's things to the room that was to be his, the boy felt as if he had known Judy for a long time. She laughed often and made it a point to include him in all their conversation. She told wonderfully interesting stories, not only anecdotes about Spring Hill's horses and riders over the years, but also many of the experiences she and Iris had shared during their girlhood together.

At last they all went to the farm. What had appeared from the road to be two or three individual barns turned out to be a series of barns attached to one another. When they stepped up on the veranda and opened the main entry door, a wave of air met them that was redolent of horses, hay, leather, saddle soap and manure, all mingled with the single most pervasive scent — that of the thick, loose, oil-treated earth composition Judy called ring dirt. It was a memorable and exciting smell and Caleb knew at once that whenever or wherever he smelled it again throughout his life, he would always associate it with this first visit to Spring Hill.

Judy led them first to her office, a tiny room dominated by a large old wooden desk upon which was a clutter of papers, ledgers and miscellaneous operational paraphernalia. Judy gestured toward the clutter with a sweep of her hand.

"Look at that," she said with exaggerated mournfulness. "I love the barn and the horses, but I really detest the paperwork it requires to keep it going. Follow me. The lounge is more conducive to relaxation."

They walked through an opposite doorway and found themselves in a spacious, rustic room furnished with several tables and their matching chairs, along with five large black leather chairs and a huge sofa of the same material. Mounted on the walls were scores of framed photographs of Spring Hill's present and past horses and riders. A large trophy case against one wall contained at least a dozen ornate silver cups, along with as many heavy bronze plaques and scores of blue ribbons. At the far end of the room was an alcove containing vending machines for candy and soft drinks. Beside them was a small table on which there was a coffee maker, its squat glass globe filled with aromatic, freshly brewed coffee. Judy indicated the latter and spoke to Iris and Warren.

"Tell you what — why don't you two have a cup of coffee here while I give Caleb the grand tour?" Without waiting for their response, she turned back to the boy and jerked her head toward an inner door. "Follow me, Caleb."

Caleb looked at his parents. They were evidently taken somewhat aback, but Warren dipped his head. "It's all right," he said. "Go along with her. We'll be right here."

The boy turned after the owner and followed her across the room and through the doorway. He very much liked her direct manner and listened carefully to what she had to say as she led him about. They passed several cats, but Judy paid no attention to them and followed a passageway to the left which took them into what she called

A-Barn. Here there was a wide central aisle flanked by ten box stalls on each side. Each compartment had a horse in it and all of them were fine thoroughbreds, some belonging to Spring Hill but the majority privately owned and being boarded. There was a good clean smell in the large room and half a dozen owners were tending to their horses, currying them with oval, rubber-toothed curry-combs, combing manes and tails and brushing the animals down until their hides literally shone under the fluorescent lighting.

Briefly — so briefly that he was gone no more than a few seconds — Caleb entered two of the horses being tended and found them in a state of enjoyment that pleased him. He hoped to have the time to enter them at greater length before long. Judy pointed out several animals with particularly colorful backgrounds or special accomplishments, then continued to lead him down the wide aisle.

At the far end of A-Barn they went through a vast sliding door into a cavernous room fully seventy by two hundred feet. Here, instead of concrete, as in A-Barn, the floor was covered with a deep layer of ring dirt. Several horses were being put through their paces by owners at one end of the barn, the hooves thudding in a pleasant muted way in the ring dirt. At the other end a class of about ten, mostly young girls in riding clothes, was being given lessons.

"This is what we call the big ring, Caleb," Judy said. "You'll see the small ring in a few minutes. In this one, which we use all year long, we can do any number of things, but mainly we use it for training horses for shows and training riders from bare fundamentals through expert handling."

She pointed toward the center where there were a number of training devices. "Those are jumps of various kinds," she said, "from the simple ground pole — which is no more than a pole lying on the ground — up through six, twelve and eighteen-inch jumps, roll tops, Rivieras, brick walls, brush boxes, single, double and triple oxers, in-and-outs, railroad-crossings . . ."

She stopped and chuckled at his look of confusion. "Don't worry about figuring them out now. By the time you're here awhile, you'll see them in use and learn which is which."

"How high do you train your horses to jump?" It was easily the twentieth question he had asked since the tour began and the barest suggestion of crow's feet showed at her eyecorners as she looked at him.

"Depends on the horse. And the rider. Here we don't often take them higher than five feet. Most often two and a half to four. We've had some fine jumpers, though. One was Grey Tark, who became Illinois State Reserve Jumping Champion. He could clear seven feet."

Caleb's eyes widened. "Do you still have him?"

"No, he's down in Tennessee now. But we do have another fine jumper here that you'll see in a little while — a gelding named Button-Eyes. He routinely takes six-foot jumps and does it with class. C'mon, let's move along."

She led him down the length of the big ring past another oversized sliding door which led to the small ring. It was a similar training room but only about half as large. They paused, looking at it for a moment, then

114

walked on to a third sliding door at the far outside end, this one leading into B-Barn. It was very similar to A-Barn, but here there were a total of forty roomy box stalls. Again there were a number of owners moving about in the central aisle, but Judy paid little attention to them and walked with Caleb to the stall closest to the door leading to three outside paddocks.

"This is Button-Eyes," she said simply, but there was a strong ring of pride in her voice. The horse was standing with his nose to the close-set iron rods above the door. She rubbed his muzzle gently. "We've raised him since he was a scrawny little runt of a colt and now he's our prize hunter-jumper. He also happens to be the Illinois State Jumping Champion."

Caleb stood on tiptoes to peer in through the vertical iron bars and felt a welling of admiration for the horse. He was a beautiful animal with black mane, tail and stockings and the rest only a slightly lighter, deep coffee color. A small patch of white hair was on his forehead.

"He's got a blaze," Caleb said, pointing, remembering the word from the caption of a picture he had seen in a library book. That picture had shown a horse with a white marking, larger than this, on its face.

"Not a blaze," the owner corrected matter-of-factly. "A blaze runs down the length of the face from forehead to nose. This mark is called a star."

"He's a beauty," Caleb breathed. "I like dark brown horses best."

Now the crinkles showed at the corners of Judy's mouth as well as her eyes. "No such thing as a brown horse, Caleb," she said. "I guess you may as well begin learning the correct terminology about a lot of things right here. Button-Eyes is a bay. What makes a horse a bay is the fact that it has black points." She saw his question forming and waved it off. "Points means the mane, the tail and the lower leg above the hoof. If they're all black it means, with few exceptions, that the horse is a bay. But there's no such thing in horse terminology as a brown horse, just as there aren't any white horses — only grays, no matter how white they look."

"How old was Button-Eyes when you got him, Judy?"

"Oh, I think he was only seven months, but he really looked bad then. That's how he got the nickname of Button-Eyes. His registered name is Jump'r Go, but he was so skinny and small when we got him that it was doubtful he'd even survive. He hadn't been cared for well and was suffering from malnutrition — both of the body and of the spirit. He looked sort of like an orange with toothpicks stuck in it for legs and the most prominent thing about him was his big dark eyes. That's where he got the nickname, and it stuck."

"You bought him from somebody else?"

She rubbed her cheek against the gelding's lips and he nuzzled her softly, obviously enjoying the contact. Caleb yearned to get inside him but held down the impulse. Judy grunted an affirmative and added: "From a trader down in southern Illinois."

"Why would you buy him if he looked so bad?"

"At the time he was sort of an afterthought thrown in as part of a deal we were making on some other horses. I think he'd probably have died if we hadn't taken him. Either that or they would have destroyed him. Anyway, he cost about two hundred and fifty dollars. That's very little for any kind of thoroughbred colt as old as he was."

"He's worth a lot more now?"

The guileless question from Caleb caused her to throw back her head and let out a peal of laughter. It was some time before she could speak and she rubbed away the tears of merriment at her eyecorners with bent knuckles. "Yes," she said, laughing some more, "you could certainly say he is. He's won more medals, silver cups, bowls and trays and blue ribbons than we know what to do with. For your information, young man, he's now worth something in the neighborhood of ninety thousand dollars."

"*Ninety thousand!*" Caleb nearly choked on the figure. It was difficult for him to imagine the sum.

"About that. Maybe even a little more."

Caleb's breath came out in a silent whistle and he stared in through the uprights with increased awe. His voice was so low that Judy could hardly hear him. "He's really a beauty. And so big!"

She nodded. "He's that, all right. Sixteen and a half hands."

"Hands?"

"Hands is the standard measurement for horses, Caleb."

"That's a funny thing to call it."

"Not really. Think about it. What do we call twelve inches?"

"A foot."

"Okay, there you are." She held out her right hand with the four fingers straight and stiff and close together, the thumb folded down on her palm. "This is what the measurement comes from," she said. "It's four inches across the broadest part of the palm. I don't know whose hand they originally measured to get it, but then I don't know whose foot they measured to arrive at twelve inches, either."

"But you said Button-Eyes was sixteen and a half hands. What does that mean? I mean, where do they measure from?"

"There's a measuring stick with a projecting moveable arm," she explained. "Something like the one you get measured with on the doctor's scale, remember? All right, one end is placed on the floor or ground and the other end, with the arm, is lowered to the withers. That's right here," she told him, touching the base of his neck, "on the hump where the neck joins the shoulders. That means Button-Eyes is five and a half feet from ground to withers. That's big, but not outstanding. Grey Tark was seventeen hands." She glanced at her wrist. "Right now the hands on my watch tell me we'd better move along."

They headed in the direction of C-Barn and once again Caleb noted the large number of cats. It seemed they were everywhere in the barns; he had lost count of how many they had seen. He asked Judy about it and she shrugged, saying they were good mousers and she didn't know exactly how many there were now, but probably in the vicinity of twenty. There were also three dogs — two German shepherds named Holly and Beau, and a large Doberman pinscher named King.

Judy Boyle walked with a swift, sure stride and Caleb found it an effort to keep up with her. He followed her into the livery, where there were doorless stalls for thirty horses, most of them with occupants, each stall with a three-foot-high chain stretched across the entry. The horses here were mainly thoroughbred, but also some quarter horses and mixtures. They were all owned by Spring Hill and used for riding lessons and ordinary rentals. Those rentals, by the half-hour or hour, were for both lessons and trail riding. The horses were bays, roans, palominos, chestnuts, grays, appaloosas and paints. Caleb thoroughly enjoyed seeing them and asked many questions. From the beginning he had plied her with questions; he continued doing so as they inspected the feed room, hayloft and tack room, then finally returned to the lounge where his mother and father were waiting. As they entered, the couple stood, looking more than just a bit disgruntled at not being invited to go on the tour and at having been kept waiting so long.

Caleb was glowing with excitement and immediately launched into a rapid-fire account of what they had seen. His admiration was strongly apparent as he described Button-Eyes, showing off his newly acquired knowledge by exclaiming, "He's a dark bay gelding, sixteen and a half hands tall, and he's the Illinois jumping champion."

"Just sixteen and a half hands, Caleb," corrected Judy with a smile. "It's not necessary to say sixteen and a half hands tall or sixteen and a half hands high."

Flushing faintly but taking no offense, Caleb rattled on with his account, but at length Judy held up her hand. "Whoa! You can tell them all about it later." She put her hand on his shoulder and looked at the Eriksons. "Quite a boy you have here. He has a good mind and I've rarely seen anyone so enthusiastic."

She smiled ruefully at them. "Now, I have to apologize for excluding you from the tour. It was intentional, not an oversight. You've told me all about Caleb, Iris. However, I wanted to find out what kind of a person he really was and long ago I learned it's almost impossible to judge a youngster by what he says or how he acts when his parents are present.

"Iris, I paid much closer attention than you thought when you first told me about Caleb — his love for animals, his identification with them, and how he acts." She was choosing her words carefully as she went on. "I share your hope that his summer here will help him and that he'll be able to . . . well, *find* himself. Now, having spent some time with him, in company with you both and, most importantly, alone, I've learned a good bit of what I needed to know."

She let her eyes rest on Caleb a moment and smiled, then looked back at Iris. "You remember I said that over the years I've taken in a good many youngsters here, usually during the summer months. They've all stayed in my home with me, using the same bedroom Caleb is in now. They've all been different, of course, some very interested in the barn and the horses, some not. In all but a few very exceptional cases they've been permitted to come to the barn only when I bring them here and even then they must stay close to me. It's very easy for someone inexperienced or careless to get hurt here, or cause damage. The stroll I took with Caleb was not unusual; I've done the same with every young person who's ever stayed with me. I make it a habit of feeling them out pretty well before I give them any degree of freedom to be near the horses."

Judy turned and looked at the boy and squeezed his shoulder. "Caleb, several times during our rounds you asked if you could spend a lot of time here in the barns, perhaps even help muck the stalls or clean floors or do other work, just for the privilege of seeing the people here caring for and training their horses, or themselves being trained in riding. It's likely there could conceivably be odd jobs you might help with now and then, but that's not the criterion for your being allowed in here unsupervised."

She paused, considering. After looking at Iris and Warren a moment, she nodded to herself as if having reached a decision and looked back at the boy. "You're welcome to enter the barns at any time, with or without me. However, there are a few important ground rules. If you break any of them — even in the smallest degree — the privilege will be rescinded. Understood?"

At his nod, she continued: "All right, these are the rules: You must either let me know or else check in with whoever's in the office first any time you come. No entering of any box stall at any time without permission. That's *very* important. Even with permission, there must be a member of the barn staff present. You may watch any activity you care to, but you must stay out of the way at all times. No teasing the horses, ever! No picking up or petting the barn cats; they're not pets, they're only here to catch mice. No feeding of any horse — not even apples or orange peels or sugar cubes — without permission; even owners are not allowed to give them hay, horse-feed or grain. That's our job here. Incidentally, you must never give a horse sugar in the first place. They love it, but it's a stupid thing to do because it's not good for their health. Finally, there must be no running, yelling or screaming — or even loud talk — in the barn or anywhere around the horses, even when they're outside. And," she added, a twinkle coming into her eyes, "when you're in the barn, no horseplay."

Caleb agreed to the restrictions with alacrity. The four of them chatted a few minutes more until Warren glanced at his watch and made a surprised little sound.

"Had no idea it was this late," he said. "We've really got to get going. Iris and I still have a lot to do — last-minute packing and making sure everything's in good shape. We won't have any time in the morning. Early flight tomorrow and we'll have to leave home at least a couple of hours before that."

They strolled out to the parking lot together and as they reached the station wagon and stopped, Judy spoke to them a final time. "Caleb's going to be just fine here. I'm very impressed with him and there's something I think you should know. Of all the youngsters I've had here, not one has ever before been allowed to come and go at the barn as he chooses. Even members of the barn crew aren't permitted to loiter or go into areas where they don't belong. I've made an exception in his case, not because it may help him overcome any problems you may feel he has, and certainly not because we're friends and this gives him special status. It's because I see a great deal in him that you two might just possibly be too close to really appreciate fully. He has intelligence, curiosity and an unusual degree of sensitivity. I also think he's a very responsible young man. I'm banking on it."

Caleb was glowing at what she said and determined to

live up to her expectations in the fullest. Yet, despite the pleasantness of Judy Boyle and her confidence in him, despite the attraction he was feeling for the barn and the horses, the final goodbyes with his parents were very painful. Though he disguised it well, there remained within him a strong resentment and feeling of rejection, along with a resurgence of loneliness that was not mitigated by the tears his mother shed, or by the unnatural huskiness in his father's voice or their warm embraces. He watched the departure of the station wagon with a great ache inside and with the continued deepseated conviction that he was uprooted and adrift, not really needed or loved by anyone.

Chapter 8

WITHIN TWO WEEKS of his arrival at Spring Hill Farm, Caleb had become a very familiar figure, likely to be encountered almost anywhere. At first he remained close to Judy at her request, going with her to the barn each morning and becoming her shadow during the rounds she would make, saying little and observing much.

Sometimes they lunched together at her house, but it was quite evident that she became edgy at the time this consumed and far more often he found himself having a hurried sandwich with her in the lounge or her office, delighted by the things she told him but increasingly sensing he was impinging on her time. He welcomed the chores she had given him to do — a regular schedule of helping to clean the broad aisles bisecting the stalls, climbing into the loft and tossing down hay bales to be loaded on a rubber-tired wagon for distribution to the horses, feeding the dogs and cats and generally helping with clean-up. But he remained very lonely most of the time.

Judy was very busy running the operation and she actually had little time to devote to him exclusively. Understanding this, he tried to help by gradually keeping more and more to himself. With increasing frequency he came to the barn alone, usually on his bike, completed his appointed tasks methodically and well, and scrupulously obeyed the rules Judy had laid down for him.

Dutifully, he kept out of the way while absorbing the essences of the big operation. Although he actually had little real interest in learning to ride, he very much enjoyed watching the horses being groomed or trained and watching new riders — usually young people — being taught the fundamentals of equitation. He thrilled at the way more experienced riders took their horses over the jumps, both in the inside training rings and in the two spacious training rings out of doors.

The barn was more to Caleb than merely a place to see horses and riders. It provided a therapy for him, dulling the ache that still filled him over the absence of his parents. In and around the barn he could sometimes almost forget the loneliness and lingering feeling of guilt he could not explain to anyone, even himself. Vainly, agonizingly, he wished he had been a better son, one in whom his parents could have felt pride instead of irritation and embarrassment. Rather than abating, his conviction was strengthened that their lives together would never be quite the same. During daylight hours he could occupy himself enough to put aside much of the pain he felt, but at night the wrenching thoughts would overwhelm him and often he lay awake in the darkness tasting the salt of tears at his mouthcorners. Occasionally, sobs he could not control wracked him and he muffled them in his pillow. Twice on such occasions Judy had come in quietly and sat on the bed beside him, stroking his hair and kissing his cheek, murmuring words of understanding and sympathy. Not until the shuddering sobs had died away and his breath came evenly in sleep would she slip silently back to her own room.

By the end of these first two weeks, Caleb had come to know intimately every horse in the barn and he had already briefly inhabited at least half of them. Sometimes he stayed with an individual for only a few minutes, at other times for an hour or more. What amazed him most was not the things the horses could do, but their reactions to their riders. In most cases the horse knew immediately whether or not the person astride its back was a beginner or an experienced rider, and the horse's performance was often predicated on this knowledge.

Caleb found the livery horses to be generally dull. They went through their paces as expected, but had little real enthusiasm for what they were doing and were always over-eager to return to their stalls to eat or sleep. The non-livery horses were of an entirely different temperament. In many ways Caleb found their behavior very humanlike, and remembrance of the word he had looked up — anthropomorphic — made him cautious about his own interpretations of a horse's reactions to whatever was occurring. Yet as he shared their sensations it was difficult not to evaluate them in human terms. He clearly sensed within them a simple pride and enjoyment in working out and in perfecting new moves; but wasn't pride an entirely human emotion? It was sometimes difficult for him to decide which were his own sensations and which were the horse's.

Fearful that he would be discovered in his dissociated state if he allowed himself to remain for any extended period of time in the animals here at Spring Hill Farm, wild or domesticated, Caleb kept his transferences very brief at first. Only gradually did the penetrations become of greater duration. One of the first of the longer periods occurred on a day when he strolled out of the back door of the barn to a pasture and saw an attractive chestnut mare named Savage Journey standing very still as she watched the gambolings of her week-old foal.

A wisp of a smile touched the boy's lips and immediately he transferred into the foal, which was a male. The colt was racing joyously in a circle and Caleb could see the mare watching him closely. She nickered softly and Caleb felt the colt's mouth open and a shrill whinny leave his throat in response. He felt the head lift high and the little tail streaming behind as the colt galloped in a wide circle one more time, then slowed and came directly to her. Savage Journey touched soft lips to the side of his head and then rubbed her muzzle along his neck. A strong sense of well-being was in the colt and it affected Caleb, helping to lighten the gloom that had been filling his heart and mind. He realized now that he really did not care a great deal if he were observed by someone while in the trancelike state; it had been a mistake to deprive himself of the incredible joy of extensively sharing another creature's experiences like this.

He shared the tightening of the little horse's muscles as he bobbed his head twice and then moved toward Savage Journey's hindquarters. He felt the colt's forelegs spread apart somewhat and experienced the dipping of his head under his mother's belly, saw close at hand the distended udder and felt its fullness and warmth as he prodded it sharply with his nose. The colt nudged it a second time and then Caleb relished the sensation as one of the nipples was taken into his mouth. The milk sucked from her was warm and rich and the sensation of fulfillment that flooded the colt was shared by Caleb. He remembered the baby rabbits and their mother cottontail he'd inhabited and, though it had been only weeks ago, the memory seemed drawn from a far distant lifetime. The nearness of the chestnut mare was comforting. Caleb experienced the contractions of the colt's throat with the greedy swallowing. He felt the haunch of his host touched, rubbed gently, and he transferred himself into the mare.

Through the eyes of Savage Journey he could see the colt at close range, the same color as his mother, legs straddled and little hooves firmly planted. He felt the soft muzzle of the mare continue to rub against the colt's flank and nuzzle his smooth hip. Along with the mare, he felt the brief sharp pain as the colt became too enthusiastic in his nursing and nipped her, and he shared the sudden bunching of her muscles as she jerked away, felt the air expel from her lungs in a snort that became a prolonged flapping of her lips.

The brief snack had been enough for the colt. After staring quizzically at her for a moment, he broke away and galloped off. Caleb marveled at the power of the mare's muscles as she broke into a trot after her offspring, then into a gallop. Ahead, the little horse ran as if he were on stilts, legs a bit too stiff, actions a bit uncoordinated, yet running well for all of that. The mare overtook him easily and slackened her pace so that they ran side by side, not stopping until they had circled the pasture a full turn. They touched muzzles again and it was at this juncture that Caleb returned to himself.

For him, the experience had been like a coming home. He suddenly knew with an utter certainty that his wonderful ability was not a curse but a great blessing. Hereafter he would use *in*-sight whenever he chose; not flauntingly, which he knew too well would only cause problems, but judiciously, whenever and wherever the notion struck him.

Of all the Spring Hill Farm horses, Button-Eyes quickly and indisputably became his favorite. He quickly came to know the gelding far more intimately than anyone in the barn, not in a riding sense as others knew him, but in a strong knowledge of what the horse himself was like, what he preferred or disliked. Button-Eyes was so attuned to the riding of his handler — a doll-faced young woman named Allison Crane — that in many cases he could anticipate her wants and perform with no more than a bare minimum of direction. The faintest pressure of a knee would set him into motion, the slighest shift of the rider's weight would telegraph what she expected and he would do it easily and well.

When Caleb occupied the consciousness of Button-Eyes, he could experience the strong sense of fulfillment that swelled in the gelding as he soared effortlessly over jumps up to five feet, and the thrill of full use of powerful muscles as he leaped with consummate grace over fences as high as seven feet. Often the jumps called oxers were set up two or three in a row, so that they were not only high but spread apart to such extent that the horse also had to clear a span of seven or eight feet at the peak of his jump. At such times the muscles rippling beneath the taut skin would stretch to their fullest. Whenever a particularly difficult jump was perfectly executed, Caleb could share the pride with which the hooves were lifted and put down, the jaunty, self-pleased attitude that flooded Button-Eyes, reflected in his snortings and in every move he made, almost as if he were saying, "Look at what I've accomplished — am I not a magnificent animal?"

Caleb's rapidly expanding experiences within animals in the barn were not limited to the horses, however much he enjoyed them. Though he didn't touch the cats, he entered the consciousness of a number of them, prowling with them through hay mow and feed rooms in search of mice, sometimes playing with one another, occasionally fighting fiercely. Few did not bear the scars of such encounters. A casual truce existed between the cats and the three big dogs. Caleb had inhabited Holly, Beau and King often and came to know them better than the cats, simply because there was no restriction involved with them; he could pet or play with them if he desired, and he chose to do so often. The three soon welcomed him at every appearance with slowly wagging tails and lolling tongues, ready and eager to romp with him or merely to follow him around the barn in his solitary rambles.

Not unexpectedly, Caleb cared little for associating with people. He generally stayed well clear of them and quickly gained a reputation among the handlers, trainers, instructors and owners of being anything from shy or strange to surly. Even though he remained circumspect about where he allowed *in*-sight to occur, more than a few times he was discovered standing motionless or sitting against some out-of-the-way wall or partition, his eyes vacant and mouth slightly ajar, his recognition of anyone wholly absent. More often than not he went unseen during the transferences, but when, on occasion, he was encountered in such a state and failed to respond, the individual would soon edge away and before long another story of Caleb's peculiar aloofness would sweep the barn. He spoke to no one, not even Judy Boyle, about his unique talent, realizing only too well that there would be no understanding.

Soon, even while he was being accepted as rather strange, although harmless, he was equally being avoided by most people at the barn. Judy was disturbed at the stories circulating about him but nevertheless remained his champion, adamantly refusing to prohibit or limit his quiet wanderings in the barn, even though such measures had been suggested by several people. Her responses were quick and to the point: "Has he gotten in the way? Has he interfered with your work or activities? Has he harmed or otherwise bothered the animals in any way?" When the answers were always "No," she would merely cock an eyebrow at the questioner and say, "Then don't worry about it," and walk away.

Nevertheless, Judy, too, had witnessed Caleb a few

times in his vacuous state and could sympathize with the discomfort it brought to others. Though she hid it very well, she also experienced the sense of uneasiness and the inclination to avoid him — an inclination angrily thrust aside. The boy obviously had problems, as his parents had obliquely hinted to her, and ignoring them was not going to help.

Now, at the beginning of Caleb's fourth week here, she once again found him sitting as if in a trance, his back against a partition in a dim corner of B-Barn. When he didn't respond to her voice, she settled beside him and waited, observing quietly and wondering how it was possible for him to become so closed off to outside activity that he didn't even realize she was there. Judy Boyle had precious little time to spare from her work, yet she remained with him for five minutes until he stirred abruptly, turned his head and found himself looking at her. He flushed deeply and gave her an embarrassed smile.

"I'm sorry, I didn't know you were here. I was . . ." He hesitated, trying to think of an excuse that would be acceptable, thought of what his parents had accused him of so many times, then went on: "I guess I was daydreaming."

Judy smiled back and laid her hand gently on his arm. "It's all right, Caleb. You miss your parents a great deal, don't you?"

"Yes." His expression became tighter as he felt the loneliness and resentment surge up. But at the same time there was a part of his mind in which he felt that perhaps he didn't really miss them enough, and he felt guilty about that.

She patted him. "You know, it's often hard to understand, when we're young, why people are the way they
are. I guess it's because we expect more of them than we
really should. As we get older, we tend to become more
mellowed, more tolerant, and we learn to become less demanding, except maybe of ourselves." She sighed deeply.
"I guess that's not much help, but I just wanted you to
know that if you need someone to talk with, I'm available.
Maybe I can't help, but I *can* listen."

Caleb dipped his head, appreciating her concern for
him, but wishing she would just leave him alone. His
thoughts turned briefly to where he had just been, glad he
had not stayed longer. More than a quarter-hour ago he
had watched the mare named Soft-Stepper being led from
her stall by her owner, Karen Boehm. He had entered
the consciousness of the horse and gone along inside her
to the big ring, where Soft-Stepper still was now. He had
gone through paces with her as Karen had directed the
mare first into different gaits and then over a series of low
jumps. He'd been inclined to stay inside the animal even
longer, enjoying the sensation of the trim, experienced
young horsewoman astride the back, feeling the skilled
directions Karen gave and sharing the immediate responses by Soft-Stepper. Yet some undefined sense had
encouraged him to return to his own consciousness and
that was when he had found Judy beside him. She was
talking again and he returned his attention to her.

"Would you like to come with me for a little while?
There's someone here I'd like you to meet. I know you've
seen him around the barn now and then, but you've never
really been introduced."

Since Judy had several times previously mentioned

that she thought Caleb must be lonely, he suspected she was taking him now to meet someone of his own age who might become a friend. He knew of no way he could refuse gracefully, so he agreed and followed without any great enthusiasm. They walked together down the length of B-Barn, then past the school area where new riders were trained to take care of their tack and animals and taught how to saddle a horse, mount and dismount properly. At the far end they passed through a wide partition door and entered C-Barn. Here, where the livery horses were quartered, Judy led him to the stall of an appaloosa gelding named Speckles, where a short, somewhat rotund man was squatting as he inspected the horse's belly. He glanced around as they stopped in the doorway, then wheezed faintly as he stood up.

Adjusting his thick, silver-rimmed glasses with a quick gesture, the man patted the horse's flank with an air of casual familiarity. "He's doing fine, Judy. Inflammation's all gone now and it's scabbing up properly. Be as good as new in a week or so." He was referring to a long gouge along Speckles's belly, which the horse had suffered when he stumbled while taking a low jump. A splintered piece of oxer had scraped his stomach. The man glanced at the boy. "I presume this is the young fellow you were telling me about?"

Judy nodded. "This is Caleb Erikson. Caleb," she continued, looking his way, "this is Dr. Colin Patrick. He's our veterinarian."

"Just call me Doc," said the man, stepping to the stall doorway and offering his hand. "Everybody does."

Caleb accepted the hand and was surprised at the

strength of the grip. The vet had a friendly face and his broad grin exposed large, slightly crooked teeth. Caleb liked him at once. He nodded. "I'm pleased to meet you, sir."

"Doc, just plain Doc. If you say 'Sir,' I'll have to keep looking around to see who you're talking to." He studied Caleb from beneath extraordinarily heavy eyebrows like tangled mats of gray wire. "I understand from Judy here that you have quite a way with animals."

"I like them," Caleb agreed, adding: "Very much."

"Excellent. We'll get along. I like 'em, too, when they're not kicking me, biting me, or crapping on my feet. How'd you like to go along on the rest of my rounds here while I check out these broken-down nags Judy tries to pass off as thoroughbreds?"

Judy barked a scornful laugh. "Thanks a lot!" Her smile faded as she went on. "Just remember, I don't want him inside the stalls with any of the horses. He can watch whatever you're doing from the doorway. Tell you what," she added, brightening, "while you two do that, I'll take care of some other things and when you're done we can have refreshments in my office. Okay?"

"Fine." Dr. Patrick winked at the boy. "Be glad to get you out of my hair for a while. Come on, Caleb, I'll put you to work right away. You can carry my satchel."

Within half an hour, Caleb felt as if he'd known Dr. Patrick all his life. The little round man was almost never silent, his continuing chatter filled with anecdotes and little jokes about the animals he handled in a five-county area northwest of Chicago. Although trained to treat almost any animal, he specialized in livestock, horses in particular. In Lake, Cook, McHenry, Kane and DuPage counties, he had some two thousand clients and treated a total of over ten thousand horses. None of his other clients had so many horses as Spring Hill Farm and he spent a fair amount of time here, coming by on rounds at least once a week and often twice. Occasionally, such as during worming times or when a contagious malady broke out, he worked at the Spring Hill barns for five or six consecutive days.

Doc Patrick handled the horses with an assurance that bespoke many years of experience and he had a phenomenal ability to calm them when they were frightened or nervous. He touched and stroked them often, spoke softly to them and made gentle crooning noises as he worked. Even animals most difficult to handle seemed to sense that he was trying to help, not hurt, and they responded by patiently accepting his expert ministrations and rarely tried to kick or bite or knock him into the side of a stall.

Just as he had a knack with horses, so too did the vet have a knack with people. He spoke to Caleb as if he were an adult, never talking down to him. In Doc, Caleb found a kindred soul — a person who loved animals as he did — and he found himself opening up far more than he had anticipated. Though he began hesitantly, shyly, soon he was talking at length about the animals he liked and what they did, how they lived and experienced things, all the while carefully avoiding the matter of how he came by this knowledge. Impressed, Doc Patrick was not daunted by the boy's reticence to explain. His question was blunt. "How'd you come to know so much about so many different kinds of animals?"

A warning sounded in Caleb's mind and he shrugged. He tried to reply casually but instead sounded evasive. "Oh, I've watched them a lot, and read a good bit about them, too. In the library."

Doc grunted and glanced sideways at the boy, but he was wise enough not to press the issue. His rounds at Spring Hill took over three hours. During that time he closely treated five horses, made follow-up examinations on half a dozen others, and gave a brief physical checkup to another forty. At about the mid-point of the examinations, Doc spent a longer time than usual examining a medium-sized chestnut mare named Fiddlesticks.

"Been off her feed the last few visits," he murmured, more to himself than to Caleb, "but hanged if I can find out what the problem is. Doesn't appear to have anything wrong with her and goes through her paces okay, but there's definitely something not right."

While Doc busied himself inspecting her, Caleb, standing at the doorway, took the opportunity to briefly enter the consciousness of the horse. Immediately he knew that Doc's diagnosis had been correct. There was a sense not so much of anything being radically wrong, but of a vague not-rightness in the animal. Caleb strained to discover the cause. The senses of the horse were at this moment closely attuned to the vet, feeling the touch of his hands on her body as they probed and searched. Fiddlesticks turned her head, and Caleb could see through her eyes the figure of the man against her off-side, rubbing and feeling. Once, as the hands came close to a spot on the barrel of her belly, almost midway up her right side and just in front of that forward bulge of the upper hind leg called the stifle, Caleb felt the muscles tense briefly, then relax as the hands went on with their inspection, missing the most sensitive spot. The veterinarian had not noticed the tensing. Caleb returned to himself just as Doc was emerging from behind the horse, shaking his head and muttering with his puzzlement.

"I don't know," he said. "Maybe it's just my imagination. I sure can't find anything. Well, I suppose if it gets serious we'll find out soon enough."

Caleb debated with himself a second or two and then made the plunge. "At one place where you touched her, Doc," he said slowly, "I thought she acted funny."

Colin Patrick looked at him steadily over the top of his glasses. "Funny? How so?"

"Well, it seemed to me she sort of winced."

"Strange I didn't notice," the vet mused. "It was while I was touching her?"

Caleb bobbed his head. "Yes, sir . . . Doc."

"Where?"

Caleb made a half-circle motion with his hand. "Around on the other side."

Frowning, because he knew the boy hadn't moved from his position near the doorway to the stall and couldn't possibly have seen what he had done on the off-side of the horse, Dr. Patrick pursed his lips and glanced around. "Show me," he said.

Without hesitation, Caleb entered the stall, moved to the far side of the mare with Doc following him, and stopped near the animal's right hind leg. With his finger only an inch from the horse's side, he pointed to the place where her discomfort had originated.

The vet put his face close to the animal's side and

looked. There was just the faintest of swelling, so slight that without attention having been called to the location, there was no way he would have seen it. He lifted his hand and pressed his stubby fingertips to it. A slight shudder rippled Fiddlesticks's side. He probed it more firmly and the mare winced, grunted faintly and shied.

"Oho," muttered Doc, "we *do* have a little problem here, don't we?" He placed his hand on her haunch and patted the mare to calm her. "Want to get my bag, Caleb?"

The boy got the medical satchel from where it was resting on the floor near the doorway. The mare shied again and Doc's voice came from behind her. "And close the stall door while you're there, will you?"

Caleb did as he was told and when he handed the bag to the vet, Dr. Patrick eyed him a moment as if considering sending him out. He decided against it. "Stand over there," he directed, "out of the way but where you can watch. You don't get queasy if you see blood, do you?"

Caleb shook his head and the vet murmured, "Good." For a while he paid little attention to the boy, but Caleb watched him closely, torn between transferring into the horse to sense what she would feel, and remaining where he was to watch the veterinarian. He chose the latter.

From his bag the vet removed a small bottle and hypodermic syringe. He plunged the needle through the lid of the bottle and about half-filled the tube. Replacing the bottle in his bag, he turned back to the horse, gently wiped the area with a cotton swab saturated with alcohol and administered three swift injections in the flesh surrounding the faint swelling. The mare's skin rippled again but she didn't shy from him. About a quarter of the fluid remained in the syringe and now he thrust the needle in more deeply and emptied it. The mare didn't move.

"Lidocaine," he said, for Caleb's benefit. "Two percent solution, with epinephrine. A local anesthetic to numb the tissues to pain."

His next move was to take a small safety razor from his bag and shave a circular area about two inches in diameter. Again he swabbed the skin. Bending over his bag again, he emerged with some small metal clamps, a slender scalpel sealed in plastic film and a long stainless steel probe with a tiny spoon at the end. He tore away the wrapping from the scalpel and then, with a movement so swift that Caleb hardly saw it, slit the clean-shaved skin horizontally with an inch-long incision, at once staunching the flow of blood with clamps. Tossing a quick glance at the boy, he said, "Hemostats." Wiping away what blood had initially flowed, he leaned close and studied the incision. Deep inside was a hard whitish knob in the muscle tissue. It was nearly the size of a ping-pong ball and with another deft move he slit it open. This time there was no blood.

He probed the deeper incision and gave a soft grunt. "Here's our culprit. Come out of there, you little bugger." He twisted and pried with the spoon-probe, got the head of the instrument behind something and levered it out.

Caleb sucked in his breath as he saw what it was. A large grayish-white grub about half the size of his little finger hung for a moment at the edge of the incision and then fell to the floor of the stall with a faint plop. An ugly, segmented maggot, it lay there moving slightly, its body in a partial U-shape. Doc placed the heel of his shoe upon it and ground it into the green-gray papier-mâché material called Stable News, used throughout the barn to cover the clay floor of all the stalls. The crushed creature made a small greasy stain in the biodegradable paper material.

"What was *that?*" Caleb asked, finding his voice at last.

Doc was busy antiseptically cleaning and closing the incision. He replied without turning around. "Bot fly larva. Some people call 'em warble flies. When they near maturity they make a huge swelling under the skin called a warble." He turned his head and looked steadily at Caleb for a long moment before returning to his work. "They're not usually detected until the swelling gets pretty large. I've never found one in this early a stage before."

"But where does it come from?" Caleb persisted. "Does it burrow in through the skin?"

Doc shook his head. "Nope. Sometimes it burrows its way out, but not in. The adult looks something like a big horsefly, except the tail's longer. Horses and mules hate them. I've seen whole herds acting crazy and sometimes stampeding, just because one comes buzzing around their heads. It's the female fly that does that. She lays her eggs on the horse; once in a while on the nostrils or lips, but more often on the hair of the foreknees where the horse will lick them off. They're swallowed with the saliva and when they're moist and pressed against tissues in the stomach, they hatch. That's where the trouble begins. The larvae are very tiny and attach to the stomach lining, where they suck fluids from the tissues. Regular worming techniques don't always work with them. One or two will make a horse not quite well — like Fiddlesticks here — but it's hard to detect the cause. Half a dozen will sap the horse's energy so much that sometimes severe illness results. They can cause some pretty bad damage to the stomach lining and intestines, too, wherever they decide to attach."

"But if they're in the stomach," Caleb questioned, "how come this one was just under the skin?"

Doc sighed. "Well, normally they'll stay in the digestive tract for eight or ten months, molting occasionally as they get larger. Then they eventually dislodge themselves, pass out with the manure, dig into the ground to pupate for a month or more and then emerge as adults ready for business again. Once in a while, though, they take a notion to dig, like this one." He nudged the mashed bot fly maggot with the toe of his shoe. "When that happens, they burrow through the lining of the stomach or intestine and begin eating their way outward toward the skin, right through the muscle tissue. That's when they're worst. I've seen them come out in the middle of the back or even through a leg. When they get just under the skin they continue eating until they're full-sized, forming a cyst as they do — which makes the swelling or warble like the one you saw me cut open. The larger it gets, the more it consumes and the more painful and debilitating it becomes to the host. Eventually, if not detected, the larva burrows out, falls to the ground and pupates as the others do."

Dr. Patrick was putting away his equipment as he concluded. The incision had been sewn shut with four tiny stitches and daubed liberally with a medicated salve. The whole operation had not taken more than five or six minutes and Caleb was greatly impressed, both with the procedure and with Dr. Patrick's knowledge. The vet snapped his bag closed and handed it to Caleb, then squeezed the back of the boy's neck.

"Thanks for your help, Caleb. Let's finish the rounds now."

"But I didn't do anything," Caleb protested.

"Indeed you did," Doc said as they closed the stall door behind them and headed for the next stop. Caleb was sure he was going to say more, that he would ask pertinent questions about how Caleb had noticed where the trouble with Fiddlesticks was centered, but he said nothing.

The next fifteen horses examined were all perfunctory stops, with a quick check for general attitude and health. All the while the veterinarian and the boy talked, their subjects ranging from school and sports and natural history to veterinary medicine and people. When Caleb asked him if he ever treated pets, Doc shook his head.

"Rarely. It's not that I don't like to work with cats and dogs or even monkeys, snakes, birds, whatever," he said, shrugging. "It's the people. Pet owners have to be among the most difficult people in the world to deal with. They very often work themselves into terrible states over the health of their pets. Horse and cattle owners are bad enough, but spare me from pet owners. Judy Boyle's an exception as a horse owner: There aren't too many like her who'll go about their business and let me go about mine. Usually they dog your steps, becoming instant experts in subjects they know nothing about and telling you what you should or shouldn't do."

"Well, why don't you just tell them to go away?"

Doc laughed. "Sometimes I do, when they get annoying enough. Not usually, though. After all, they're the owners and they're concerned. Also, they usually have quite an investment in particular animals, apart from merely liking them. So most of the time you bite your tongue and let them feel important, if that's what they want, and forget about giving them what for. Long ago I learned that in most circumstances you have to keep your words sweet and tender — you never know when you're going to have to eat them."

As they continued the rounds, Caleb continued to help surreptitiously. Always waiting until the vet was hidden behind the horse he was checking, Caleb, standing by the stall door, briefly entered the consciousness of each one to sense what it was feeling. Most were in good health, but once again during the course of the rounds he detected a malady that the veterinarian would have missed. It occurred with a placid old bay gelding named Poor Boy. The animal was checked over quickly but thoroughly by Dr. Patrick and pronounced to be in good shape. But Caleb had entered Poor Boy and sensed something wrong with two of the hooves, especially the right rear. As the vet was about to leave the stall, the boy spoke up a little self-consciously.

"Doc, while you were checking the front hooves, he lifted up that one," he pointed, "like it was hurting him."

The vet paused and pursed his lips, looking where the boy was pointing. "I checked the hind hooves, too, Caleb, remember?"

"I know you did and I thought maybe you'd find something wrong with it. Then, when you didn't, I thought maybe I was wrong. But when you turned around just now, he did it again. So I thought I'd better . . . well . . ." His voice trailed off and he was suddenly not only embarrassed for having said anything, remembering what Doc had said about people dogging his steps and becoming instant experts, but fearful that his unusual talent would be found out.

Wordlessly, the veterinarian turned and went back to the horse, opening a small pocketknife as he did so. He faced the rear and leaned his weight against Poor Boy, at the same time lifting the leg at the ankle. Obediently the old horse shifted his weight and let the man lift the hoof.

"Looks okay, Caleb," he said, studying its underside. Ring dirt was packed solidly against the frog — the soft place at the rear of the hoof — and there was no indication of swelling or inflammation to suggest anything wrong. Now, however, as he scraped against the packed dirt with the tip of the knife, a clod broke away and immediately the vet wrinkled his nose and turned his head away, dropping the foot.

"Hmmm," he murmured to himself, "now how do we account for that?" He looked at the boy. "I'll check the other hooves more closely while I'm at it. Will you go up to the office and have them give you a bucket half-filled with warm water?"

Caleb nodded and walked away at once, holding down the impulse to run in filling the errand, mindful of Judy's strict edict against running in the barn. He had gone only about twenty yards when Doc's voice stopped him. He looked back to see the little man standing in the stall door-way.

"I'll need a stiff wire brush, too."

Caleb acknowledged with a raised hand and walked on hurriedly. In less than five minutes he was back inside the stall with the water and the brush. He gave them to Doc and then, as he had done with Fiddlesticks, closed the stall door and moved out of the way inside the stall to watch what Doc would do. It was just after Doc finished scraping off the ring dirt from the left front hoof that Judy Boyle appeared at the stall door, looking not at all pleased. Doc straightened as she entered and he made a clucking sound.

"Looks as if Poor Boy's gotten himself a case of thrush, Judy. Two hooves." The vet knelt near his satchel and removed from it a pint-sized dark green bottle. He glanced up at Caleb. "While I mix this with the warm water, take a look around and see if you can find any moisture on the floor."

Judy frowned, opened her mouth as if to say something, then closed it in a tight line without having spoken. Caleb walked along the walls of the stall. As he neared the automatic water bowl he felt the ground beneath his feet becoming softer. The metal water bowl was one of those in which there was a tongue-like lever. When the water level became low enough, the pressure of the horse's muzzle against it as it drank caused fresh water to flow in. Caleb looked it over and found that where the water pipe entered the bowl underneath there was a steady drip every few seconds.

"There's a leak here," he said.

"Oh, fine!" The exasperation was heavy in Judy's voice. "That's all we need now, to have bowls start leaking all over the barn. Well, we'll move Poor Boy into the empty, two stalls down, and get this repaired right away. I'll have someone check out the rest of the bowls. Is it bad?"

Dr. Patrick shook his head. "Not really. Hind one's more advanced than the front, but only now getting a good start. It's lucky we caught it when we did."

He had placed the bucket of mixed fluid under the left front hoof of the old gelding and was scrubbing the bottom surface with the wire brush. The odor of strong disinfectant filled the stall, but it couldn't entirely mask the revolting stench rising from the hoof being scrubbed. The more of the packed dirt that was removed from the bottom of the hoof, the worse the stench became. By the time he had the frog fully exposed, Doc was breathing erratically, holding his breath as long as he could while working on the hoof, then turning his head to exhale and inhale in great gasps.

"What's thrush?" Caleb asked, his stomach churning.

Judy answered for Doc, her tone level, mechanical. "It's a bacterial infection of the hoof."

"Called *Ceropherus necropherus*," Doc muttered.

Judy went on with hardly a pause. "It attacks the frog, where the hoof is softest. Usually comes from the animal standing on a damp piece of ground too long. It's not very pleasant."

With the hoof thoroughly washed, the vet sprinkled some powder from a foil packet liberally on the infected area and explained that it was a sulpha medication that would quickly clear up the problem. He sent Caleb to get a double handful of ring dirt and by the time the boy returned with it, the vet had finished cleaning and medicating the right rear hoof as well. The stench in the stall was even worse than before. Doc took the ring dirt from Caleb, mixed it with a little fresh water from the automatic bowl and molded a couple of lumps of firm mud, each about the size of a golf ball. When he lifted the rear hoof again, Judy helped in holding the raised leg steady. The veterinarian sprinkled a little more of the sulpha powder over the frog and then used his strong stubby thumbs to mold one of the mud balls firmly into place over it, packing it until the bottom of the hoof was caked as it had been before he started. The whole process was repeated with the front hoof.

They moved the gelding two stalls down and as they did so, Judy glanced at Caleb and then at the vet. Her expression was still pinched. "I thought you agreed," she told the man, "that you wouldn't take him into the stalls with you."

Doc shrugged. "Turns out it was a good thing I did. He's been of help, as you saw."

Judy was not pleased. "That's not the point! I specifically asked you not to let him enter a stall any farther than the doorway and —"

"Which," the vet interrupted, "is exactly where he's been most of the time. He hasn't come in farther than that of his own volition." Doc's words carried an edge of irritation. "He's only done what I've asked him to do."

"Well, I really meant it." Her voice was flat, her manner implacable. "I don't want him in the stalls. I'm glad he was of help, but I don't want him in any stalls unless *I* specifically say that's where he can go." She turned and pointed a finger at the boy. "Do you understand that?"

Caleb's expression was wooden. "Yes."

"Doc," she continued, "I appreciate all the care you give my horses. I pay dearly for it, too. But in these barns, what I say goes. I do not intend to have him — or the horses! — getting hurt." She didn't give him a chance to reply. "I'll go get someone to work on that water bowl right away, and have the others inspected."

She whirled around and strode away while the man and boy watched without moving until she turned the corner at the far end of the barn. Then Doc looked at Caleb and grinned a little sheepishly.

"I think I got you into trouble," he said. "I'm sorry. I didn't mean to."

"That's okay. It was my fault as much as yours. I knew I wasn't supposed to go inside, but I really wanted to watch what you were doing."

Colin Patrick chuckled. "I'll take that as a compliment, although I have to say I'm a little nonplused at the way you detected the problems with Fiddlesticks and Poor Boy. You interest me. Are you doing anything in particular tomorrow?"

"No."

The vet smiled broadly and began walking toward the office, Caleb falling into step beside him. "Good. How'd you like to go on rounds with me tomorrow to some of the other farms around here?"

The boy's eyes widened. "Sure! I'd love it!"

"Excellent. Check it out with Judy and see if it's all

right with her. She has my home number. I'm going to have to forgo our refreshments for now. Running late. If there's any problem, have her give me a call this evening. Otherwise, I'll pick you up tomorrow morning at the house at seven o'clock, okay?"

"Okay!" Caleb's eyes were sparkling and it was only with the greatest of difficulty that he refrained from breaking loose with a whoop of joy.

Chapter 9

IT WAS DIFFICULT for Judy Boyle to believe that Dr. Colin Patrick had actually invited Caleb to accompany him on his rounds to other farms. At the dinner table that evening she listened with interest as he told her about the day's activities in the barn. She was amused at his exuberance over Doc's skill, but then she became serious.

"Caleb, I'm sorry I became upset in the barn today, but it is very important for you to understand that it is strictly prohibited for you to go into any stall where there is a horse. You must remember that it's only because I trusted you that I gave you the freedom to roam the barns, and you agreed to the stipulations I laid down. One of those was your promise that you would never enter any stall without my permission."

"But I was with Doc! He asked me to do things with him, to help him, and that's what I was doing."

"I understand that," she said firmly, "but the fact remains that you did go into the stalls. It was up to you to reiterate the fact that you were not allowed to enter them. Did you do that?"

Caleb looked at his plate and his voice became low. "No."

"Then you see," she continued reasonably, "you weren't being very fair to him, either. You placed him in an awkward position and I'm sure he wasn't very pleased with that."

"But he *knew* I wasn't supposed to go inside. You had told him that yourself. He *still* wanted me to help him. Anyway, he didn't get mad at me. He didn't get mad at anyone."

"Caleb, darling, listen to me and try to understand that there's a good reason for the rules. I have a huge operation to run and I have to be able to count on the people who are here to do as I say. It doesn't matter whether it's a trainer or a student, a barn hand or Doc Patrick or you. The rules are not to be ignored by anyone. I don't want you getting hurt and neither do I want the horses becoming excited and perhaps hurting themselves. Did you know that a few years ago we lost a valuable horse because of someone's carelessness?"

"No."

"Well, we did. One of the barn crew, a boy of about eighteen — his name was Larry — wasn't careful while loading some horses to go to a show. We were taking along a four-year-old gelding named Chieftain, that we'd just bought for around twenty thousand dollars. Larry was paying more attention to a class of girl riders than to the job he was supposed to be doing and he didn't secure the ramp properly to the horse trailer. As he was putting the gelding in, the ramp slipped. It wasn't a very far drop, no more than a couple of feet, but one of Chieftain's front legs got broken and we had to destroy him. It was a terrible loss. I fired Larry, but that didn't correct the damage. The point is, the barn is never a place for carelessness or forgetfulness or disobedience. Several of the horses we have now are worth over fifty thousand dollars each, and, as you know, Button-Eyes is valued at ninety thousand dollars. I can't afford to have my instructions disobeyed where such valuable animals are concerned."

She paused and blew at a tendril of hair that had become dislodged and hung across her eye. "Enough! I'm lecturing and don't really mean to. I just wanted you to know why I got upset. I ask you to solemnly promise me now that you'll obey this rule hereafter."

"I promise," he told her, sincerely sorry about what had happened.

"Good boy," she smiled. "Now, suppose you tell me the rest of what happened between you and Doc after I stormed off."

That was when Caleb broke the news that Dr. Patrick had invited him along on his rounds to other farms tomorrow. Judy was so surprised she called Doc to confirm it and listened for quite a while as the veterinarian spoke. At length she said, "Okay, he'll be ready for you at seven." She returned to the table chuckling. "Well, you certainly made an impression on Doc. I've never heard him so effusive about anyone before. Evidently he thinks you're something of an asset to have with him."

Caleb was not only ready earlier than necessary, he had taken up his vigil on the little front porch by six-thirty. The next half hour dragged interminably for him. A hawk sailed past overhead and Caleb considered entering it, then decided against it for fear he'd be away from himself when Dr. Patrick arrived. A crow landed in the top of the big maple at the head of the driveway and Caleb longed to enter it, but did not. A young rabbit hopped into the yard and paused to nibble some clover. Caleb watched it enviously until it disappeared into the hedgerow. Robins and sparrows flitted about; a meadowlark rose from the deep prairie grass across the road, landed briefly on a telephone wire and then returned to the grass; a squirrel chattered incessantly at a bluejay in a large oak a short distance away. All of nature seemed to be beckoning to Caleb, but he resisted the temptation and finally, a few minutes before the hour, Dr. Patrick's dusty white van turned into the driveway.

Judy came out to see them off and Doc promised to have Caleb back late in the afternoon. Then they were off, driving eastward through Algonquin and then on the county line road toward Barrington. The area Dr. Patrick was covering today included northern Cook County and southern Lake County, and they stopped most often at horse farms. There were no emergencies except for a holstein cow on one farm that had severely torn a teat when she became entangled in barbed wire. Dr. Patrick quickly and expertly sewed up the wound.

In most cases the calls were more or less routine and the problem with a specific animal quite obvious, the treatment fairly cut and dried. The most common problems seemed to be respiratory ailments, sometimes treated with an ingestible medicine and occasionally with injection of an antibiotic, but most often left alone to run their brief courses under close watch for possible complications. Where injuries were concerned, the most frequent were lacerations or punctures from exposed nails in stalls and bruises from being jostled during transportation in trailers. Now and then the horses had to be treated for injuries resulting from bites and kicks suffered from other horses. Caleb marveled at the skilled manner Doc had with the animals and how they seemed to know intuitively that he was on hand to help them. Rarely did one of them show any degree of irritation or grow excited or upset at his examinations, probings and treatments.

It was in those cases where the problem with an animal was not specifically known that Caleb would become more interested. The farmer or horse breeder would scratch his head and say something like, "Well, I don't really know what's wrong with her, but there's definitely something wrong. She's just not acting right. You know, off her feed and sluggish. . . ." In such cases, as Doc carefully examined the animal, Caleb would briefly use *in*-sight to try to pinpoint the problem area. Sometimes it was a stomach ailment or muscle spasm. Occasionally it was a pulled tendon or even a cracked or broken bone. In such circumstances Caleb would casually point out something externally that would put the veterinarian on the right track for correct diagnosis and treatment of the problem. Although occasionally the vet would give Caleb a long speculative look, the boy was sure the animal doctor did not have the least suspicion of how he was arriving at his casual suggestions about where the trouble lay.

Despite the fact that it was what Doc apologized for

being "a very mundane day," Caleb found it fascinating. He also was fearful that it was a one-time affair and that he would never again be invited to go on the vet's rounds with him. In that he was very mistaken. When Doc dropped him off at five o'clock and Caleb thanked him for being permitted to go along, the vet asked if he'd like to go again the day after tomorrow, when he'd be making stops in the area of Antioch and Lake Villa in northern Lake County. Assuredly, Caleb did.

During the three weeks that followed, Caleb accompanied the veterinarian at least three times a week. With ever-growing confidence, inspired by Doc's eagerness to have his views, the boy would "suggest" where problems lay when Doc could not detect satisfactory external symptoms. The difficulty for Caleb lay in attributing the problem he pinpointed inside the animal to some outward manifestation so the man would not suspect anything unnatural. But Caleb could see no sign that Dr. Patrick thought there was anything abnormal about his flair for diagnosis. As time progressed, the vet even ceased asking the boy what he had seen that led him to suggest where the problem originated.

Once a horse kicked hard and only an adroit move on the part of the vet saved him from possibly being injured. As they drove from that place on to their next stop, they discussed the incident and laughed together over the way the vet had leaped out of the way. Then Doc sobered somewhat and his words became serious.

"You get accustomed to anticipating kicks and bites," he said. "Especially kicks. You'd better, or you'll be laid up with your own injuries half the time. Or else dead."

He reflected a moment and then shook his head. "That's one of the main things Judy was considering when she said you had to stay out of the stalls, Caleb. A horse's hooves are lethal weapons if he wants 'em to be. Sometimes they even hurt themselves. I've seen more than one case where a horse was bitten on his belly by a horsefly and reacted automatically with a kick that nearly caved him in. Hematomas like you wouldn't believe! So, you learn to anticipate and be ready to move."

In such casual conversation as this during rounds, Caleb quickly picked up a surprising store of information and veterinary lore from the man. They lunched together often at a place called the Kelsey Road House a few miles northwest of Barrington, or on the outdoor patio of a restaurant called Hackney's at Lake Zurich. They talked a great deal as they ate and Colin Patrick was gradually gaining a deeper insight into this unusual boy who sat across from him.

One day as they sat together at a table overshadowed by a huge umbrella on Hackney's patio, watching the ducks as they dabbled in the pond and begged tidbits of breadcrusts and French fried potatoes from the patrons, Caleb became more ebullient than usual. He also let himself become more retrospective than at any other time since their association began. He talked about his parents and about Zion and Mike Marlett while the vet listened closely. He spoke of Miss Olstrohm at East School and of the beaches along Lake Michigan and the marshes between the town and the lake. He discoursed at length about the birds and mice, fish and frogs he had observed there and it was not at all difficult for the vet to see how the boy became tense when he spoke of his relationships with people, and how he became so much more at ease when he spoke of plants and wildlife.

"Have you always been lonely, Caleb?"

The abruptness of the question took Caleb off balance and he stopped chewing as he thought it over. Then he hunched his shoulders. "I guess so."

"Why? Do you feel that people don't understand you?"

"Yes, sometimes. Most of the time, I guess."

"Have you ever really tried to talk to them? I mean have you ever made an effort to open up and let them inside, right where you live?"

"Sure I have! But when I did, they wouldn't listen." The words came out in a rush. "Most of the time they wouldn't believe what I was saying. Or else they just didn't listen, even if they pretended to."

Doc's voice was gentle. "Are your mother and father like that?"

"I . . . guess they are." The sense of guilt came back in a rush. "Not all the time," he amended hastily. "But when it's really important, they never seem to hear me."

The veterinarian slowly turned his coffee cup in the saucer and spoke without looking up. "What was it you've brought up to them that was important that they wouldn't listen to?"

Caleb withdrew at once. "Nothing," he mumbled, then changed that by adding, "Just things." He hunched his shoulders. "I don't know."

Doc said nothing and the silence drew out and became uncomfortable. Caleb sat with his head down, hands in his lap, fingers nervously interlocking and then releasing.

The vet hiked his chair a little closer and reached out, placing his hand on Caleb's arm.

"Do you miss them a great deal?" he asked softly.

Caleb nodded without looking up and felt a surge of anger at the hot tears that had begun sliding down his cheeks. When he did lift his head and look directly at the vet, his voice was louder than he meant it to be. "But I *don't* miss them, too! Sometimes I think it would be better if they never came back. They don't care about what I think or say. They always make me feel like I'm doing everything wrong and causing problems for them. I don't *mean* to! I just want them to *listen* to me sometimes." He broke off, sobbing heavily.

Dr. Patrick waited a long while, not speaking until the sobbing had abated. His words were quiet. "Caleb, everyone wants to be listened to, especially if he has something important to say. This involves a few problems. First of all, it's often hard to find someone who really listens. People are far more interested in talking about themselves and their own concerns than in listening.

"Second, you'll find that quite often people don't think the same things are important that you do; even if they act as if they're listening, they're really not. Unfortunately, we run into this sort of thing all our lives. Eventually we become more or less accustomed to it. We also tend to grow more selective in the people we open up to, because it's futile and humiliating to try to put something across to someone who doesn't care and simply won't listen."

Caleb was looking at the man closely now, afraid of believing there could be an adult who was so understanding of what he felt. He rubbed his eyes with the heel of one hand and was about to speak when Doc went on. What he said struck Caleb with even greater impact.

"I expect you probably feel a little guilty over your parents taking their big trip this summer without you, but you don't know exactly why. You've wanted them to understand you and they haven't and you feel if they had, they wouldn't have gone away without you. You blame yourself for failing to make them understand, but, Caleb, let me tell you something: Chances are they never will fully understand. If there is a fault to be found, or guilt to be borne, it is probably theirs, not yours."

Dr. Patrick held up a hand, warding off the comment Caleb was about to make. He shook his head. "Please, wait. Let me finish. I'm well aware that I don't know your parents, but I do know you. In the past weeks I've watched you closely . . ." he paused, looking at the boy directly, ". . . and often when you didn't suspect I was watching. Though I don't know your parents, I know something about them that you don't. I have no doubt they love you in their own way, but because they won't listen to you, they really know very little about you and they evidently have no conception whatever of your potential — or your remarkable sensitivity.

"I don't think that's too unusual," he went on. "Probably a fair percentage of parents never fully suspect the potential of their own children and so they don't encourage them, don't help them to develop the potentialities they have. Some of the young ones find their way in spite of this and become what they really should become, no matter how many hurdles they have to surmount. A lot don't, and they become what they thought their parents wanted them to become. Often they wind up going through their lives never completely happy, never completely satisfied, locked into jobs they don't care about but are unable — and finally unwilling — to change, unable to break the mold into which they've been cast. They also go through their lives carrying a load of guilt that was imposed upon them without their even suspecting it, by the only ones who could do such a thing — those they love most. And they get to feeling, deep inside, that they've never been true to themselves, and in that way they add even more to their burden of guilt."

He shook his head and smiled wryly. Gulping down the last few swallows of his coffee, he set the cup down and went on. "I got carried away. You'd think I was a psychologist instead of a vet. Anyway, have you been able to understand what I've said?"

Caleb wasn't sure. He knew that what Doc was saying was terribly important; further, that no one had ever talked to him this way before. He was grateful for having a rare privilege bestowed upon him, even though he could not precisely define what it was. And so, while not completely comprehending the vet's words, he nevertheless nodded and said, "I think so."

"Caleb, let me ask you a question. Take your time answering it, if you want to. In fact, you don't have to answer at all if you'd rather not. Have you ever thought very much about what you want to do with your life? What you want to be?"

Caleb had thought about it many times. The boys he knew at school talked about it at times; mostly they yearned to be astronauts or doctors or big league pitchers, lawyers or firemen or detectives or any number of professions they considered to be glamorous or productive of more-than-average income or just plain interesting and fun. But all Caleb could ever remember wanting to do was the thing that made him happiest and fulfilled him most — entering the consciousness of living things and observing through their eyes what they were seeing, experiencing. But how could he ever tell others this? It seemed that no one could really understand it, and that certainly wasn't their fault: It was something outside their experience or comprehension. But to Caleb it was the very essence of life.

He shrugged his shoulders slightly — a gesture that had always irritated his mother. "I don't know for sure," he said, not wanting to lie and yet equally not knowing how to phrase the truth. "I like being around animals."

Doc tugged casually at one of his bushy eyebrows, looking thoughtful. "How would you like to become a veterinarian?"

Caleb felt his pulse quicken. "I never really thought about it until I met you and saw what you were doing. Lately I've wondered if it might be possible." That was an understatement. Obviously, entering the consciousness of animals was hardly a profession, hardly a way to make a living. Now he had discovered through his association with Dr. Patrick that perhaps his *in*-sight ability could have a purpose. Perhaps if he were to become a vet and work closely with animals that needed help, he could be of value.

Doc signaled the waitress for another cup of coffee and

waited to speak until she had poured it and left. "It's definitely possible, Caleb," he said, emptying a packet of artificial sweetener into the coffee and stirring it. "You have a remarkable affinity with animals. Maybe amazing is the more proper word. I've never encountered anything quite like it. You possess a phenomenal natural talent for diagnosing illness and injury in animals. That alone could be an asset beyond compare to you if you were to become a vet."

A flush of pleasure filled Caleb at the words. He felt a strong gratitude toward this plump little man who spoke to him in so straightforward a manner. At the same time, he experienced a niggling of fear that in pointing out to the vet what was wrong with certain animals, he might have given himself away. His stomach muscles tightened at the thought. He wished Doc would get off that particular subject and so he said nothing. It didn't help.

"How do you do it?"

Caleb stopped smiling and pretended not to understand. "Do what?"

The corners of Colin Patrick's mouth twitched as he controlled an impulse to smile. He answered patiently. "How do you so accurately detect what's wrong with an animal?"

The boy hunched his shoulders, still saying nothing, more uncomfortable every moment.

"Look, Caleb," Doc said, pulling his chair closer yet, "I'm not trying to pry." He paused and shook his head. "No," he contradicted himself, "that's not true. I am prying, but I think it's very important. I've seen you become . . . well, 'apart' would be a good word. I've seen you become apart briefly, as if your body were only a shell standing there and your consciousness had gone elsewhere. Then you're back and you make a suggestion about what's wrong with a horse or a cow or some other animal and it's invariably correct. How, Caleb? How do you do it?"

Caleb's lips tightened in a resolute line and he shook his head faintly. His eyes were on the empty plate again.

"You don't want to talk about it, do you?" At another barely perceptible headshake by the boy, he went on: "You've been hurt in this respect before, I think. You've trusted someone and that someone ridiculed you or betrayed your trust. I wouldn't do that, Caleb. I wouldn't do anything to hurt you in any way. Most certainly I would never laugh at you or become scornful. But I do understand your not wanting to talk and I won't press you on it. Maybe someday, when we get to know one another even better, we can talk about it."

Caleb lifted his head and looked the veterinarian directly in the eyes. The vow he had made to himself never to tell anyone again was put aside. His stomach was churning but his words were calm. "We can talk about it now. I can get inside animals."

He waited fearfully for the reaction of disbelief, the amusement or laughter or condescension that he knew would send him running out of the restaurant, not knowing or caring where he would go. There was no such reaction.

"How?" Doc asked.

"I just decide to get inside their heads and I'm there."

"And coming back?"

"The same way."

"What happens when you get inside an animal? What do you do?"

"Nothing. I mean *I* don't do anything. But I know everything the animal is doing — what it's seeing or smelling or hearing. I can taste whatever it tastes and when it makes a sound, it's like I'm making it. I feel everything it feels."

"What can you make the animal do?"

"I can't *make* it do anything. I've tried, but I can't. I'm just there, that's all."

The veterinarian digested this a moment in silence and took a sip of the now tepid coffee. "How long do you stay inside?"

"As long as I want to. Or as short. I was in a screech owl all night one time."

"God, that's marvelous," the man breathed. He frowned as a thought struck him. "What if you're in an animal and it gets hurt . . . or even killed?"

"That's happened. When it does, I just transfer into something else." He told the vet then of the instance with the fly and the Venus flytrap and it was clear that Dr. Colin Patrick was astounded.

"Obviously," the vet said, when Caleb had finished the story, "you've been inside horses and cows, an owl and a fly and a Venus flytrap. What else?"

Caleb was warming to the subject. With the self-imposed restraints gone, the words rushed to be free as he told of the wide variety of birds, mammals, insects, fish, amphibians and reptiles he had entered, and of the trees and plants his consciousness had penetrated.

"Have you gone into plants a great deal?"

"Not really. I've gone into a lot, but animals are more

fun. Plants don't do very much. It's a nice feeling being inside them and all, but they don't do much. Birds are best. It's terrific to fly with them and feel the air going past and see the ground below. I like to fly with them in flocks, too."

Caleb then went on to tell of how he had told Mike Marlett about his talent, and about the anguish it had caused him when Mike told their classmates. He told about the tree in the storm and the dragonfly metamorphosis. Throughout the recitation, Colin Patrick sat and listened as if mesmerized.

"How long," he asked as the boy paused, "have you been able to do this?"

"How long? I've *always* done it. I can't remember not doing it."

"How do you determine what's wrong with an animal when it's sick or hurt?" The veterinarian's voice betrayed his excitement.

Caleb's brow furrowed. "I'm not sure," he admitted. "It's just that when I get inside, there's a feeling that something's wrong or that it hurts. Then all of a sudden I know where it's coming from. I don't usually know what's causing it, but I do know where something's wrong and how bad it feels."

Doc shook his head, his eyes dancing. "By golly," he chortled, "this is incredible! I've got to see it happening again. I've got to watch it close up." He shot a swift glance at his watch and stood up. "Come on. We're more than half an hour behind schedule now. Let's get on with the rounds." He put his arm around Caleb as they left the restaurant. "Now you can get inside those animals we're looking at without trying to hide it from me. I warn you, though, I'm probably not going to stop asking you questions for a week!"

Dr. Colin Patrick lived up to his word, and whatever reservations or skepticism he may have harbored soon vanished.

Chapter 10

Y THE END of their fourth week of going on rounds together, Caleb Erikson and Dr. Colin Patrick were firm friends. The veterinarian's clients were becoming accustomed to seeing the boy carrying the big black satchel and remaining close to the vet during his examination and treatment of their horses or other livestock. The short round man and the boy often held murmured conversations near the animals and the owners were more than just mildly impressed at the ability of the vet to discern and treat problems the animals were having which no one, until then, had detected.

It was during the fifth week, however, that the two did not see one another at all. The reason was that Dr. Patrick came down with a severe cold; his wife insisted it was influenza, though the vet knew it was not. The malady kept him in bed for three days and feeling rotten for the next four as he caught up on office and laboratory work he had let slide for too long.

Caleb was very much at loose ends during this period, yearning for the time when Doc would be well enough to resume his normal rounds and take Caleb with him. The boy read and reread the cards and letters he had received from his parents, intrigued by the experiences they reported and fascinated by the colorful foreign stamps and exotic postmarks. Abruptly he found himself harboring an unsettling ambivalence with respect to their planned return in ten days. While he still missed them and was looking forward to being reunited, he didn't want to leave Dr. Patrick and Spring Hill Farm. He was disturbed by the realization that it was now the downhill side of August, which meant that before long he would have to return to Zion to reenter East School for the eighth grade.

At noon on Friday, Judy Boyle summoned Caleb to her office in the barn and reported that she had just received a telephone call from Dr. Patrick. The veterinarian had told her that he would be resuming his regular rounds on Monday morning and wanted Caleb to accompany him. Caleb was more than pleased and, knowing their time together would largely be spent with the livestock and horses of the surrounding countryside, he decided to use the time until then to do something he had largely neglected since becoming closely associated with Doc.

Throughout the remainder of Friday, all of Saturday and Sunday until late afternoon, he roamed the fields behind Spring Hill's barns, moving slowly from place to place, pausing beside a little brook and at an old dead tree, sitting on a rock alongside a fence row, leaning against a post beside a woodlot. At each place he entered some different living creature and, as always, the experiences were exhilarating beyond most things he experienced through his own senses.

The grasshopper he entered chewed methodically on a corn leaf just below the tassel and he tasted the sweet juices of the plant along with the insect. Then the grasshopper abruptly moved beneath the leaf and clung motionlessly in response to the shadow of a passing bird, and Caleb left it and moved on.

When a gaudy cock pheasant emerged hesitantly from a field of soybeans and broke into a run with head and tail high, he was with him, feeling the strength of the legs carrying him toward the protective cover of the fence row. He moved into the tangle of underbrush with the bird and shared the sensations as it paused, listening and watching. When certain there was no danger, the pheasant ducked through the interlocking branches and vines and settled comfortably on the ground. The boy abandoned the bird at that point.

He became one with a female garter snake clad in the dull tatters of an old skin and remained with her as she slid through a bramble, deliberately rubbing her head against sharp, curved thorns until at last one snagged and held the skin at her upper lip. She shoved forward with slow steady strength, and he felt her old skin lift and peel back until the entire head had been pulled free of the outgrown garb; shared the sinuous twistings of the reptile as she brushed against more briars which hooked and held the colorless skin as more of it came free behind the head; experienced the delicious sensation of peeling back the full skin, of moving forward with even more determination and simply crawling out of the used garment until, inside out, it hung ghostlike from the brambles, tissue thin and rubbery soft but gradually drying, and with torn parts of it wafting in the faint breeze, no more now than the mute memory of a snake that had passed. And, clad in her bright and shiny brand new yellow-striped gown, the snake slid beneath a broad piece of bark and curled up to rest from her exertions, at which point Caleb left her.

The boy lived during the weekend in a melange of sensual sharings, without ever becoming sated. He tasted fresh warm milk with a calf he briefly inhabited, and shared with a huge old sow her greedy crunching of hard field corn off its dry red cob; he ate the warm tender flesh of a young rabbit after sharing the hunt inside a wily, well-scarred tomcat; swallowed a noisy horsefly which alighted too close to a camouflaged bullfrog on the shore of a farm pond; gulped down a large caterpillar snatched off its maple leaf by a red-headed woodpecker he had joined.

He felt the exciting rush of the air as he dove with a marsh hawk from a great height; shared the cozy warmth of a collie's underside as she snuggled the pup he was inhabiting, felt the comfort of being with his wriggling litter-mates close around him, and reveled in the gentle laving of her tongue as she cleansed him; he measured the length of a twig while inhabiting an inchworm and then lowered himself to the ground on a silken strand extruding from the rear of its body; he lived the pain of a warbler that flew into a picture window and very nearly broke its neck.

He watched the flight of a falcon through the fearful eyes of a pigeon, studied the movements of a lumbering beetle through the curious eyes of a kitten, observed the swaying and bending of a bed of colorful asters through the multifaceted eyes of a honeybee, and examined an intriguing hole in the ground with the eyes of a raccoon.

Through the ears of a red fox he heard the piercing little death shriek of the mouse it had just caught, and the roar of a passing truck through the ears of a grackle picking up scattered grain along the edge of a road; he heard the low hissing growl of an opossum through the ears of a somewhat fearful yapping puppy that had discovered it beneath an old shed.

He caught the scent of burning grass in the nostrils of a field mouse as it plunged into a burrow, the aroma of newly mown hay in the nostrils of a tired old mare gazing longingly through a paddock fence to an adjoining field where timothy was being baled.

In-sights were not only endless, they were endlessly differing and Caleb never tired of sharing them with a progression of hosts, feeling most alive and in tune with both nature and himself as he absorbed the experiences. This was what he loved most in the world. More than that, it was what he *needed* and he knew he would never be completely happy doing anything else.

At length, late in the afternoon on Sunday, he strolled back toward the barn. In a pasture on the other side of the white board fence he was following, a grazing blood bay mare, heavy with foal, lifted her head and watched as first he approached and then paused to regard her. An instant later, through her eyes, he saw himself standing with one hand on the top rail, one foot on the bottom. When he no longer moved or made any sound, she turned her gaze back to the ground and resumed cropping the low-growing grass. Caleb shared the sensations as her flanks shivered to dislodge flies and the whisking of her long black tail for the same purpose. The pasture grass, drier than it had been earlier in the summer, nevertheless had a good taste and he could feel the crinkly texture of it as the massed blades were crushed between the large molars.

Caleb felt a movement of the heaviness within her body cavity, remembered that she was pregnant and immediately transferred himself into the fetus. It was a colt, only a week from birth and very active. The long legs doubled together like jackstraws, periodically strove vainly to straighten and the large head occasionally moved from side to side within the limited confines. The membranous amniotic sac, initially roomy, in which the fetus had more or less floated, had now become a less-than-spacious prison in which he was uncomfortable insofar as movement was concerned. Comfort was still there, of course, in other ways: the warm darkness, the sense of security, the lack of hunger pangs. All these were symptomatic of the only existence the unborn colt had ever known and he was not discontent with them. Only where space was concerned did a sense of unrest fill him. He no longer floated, but lay heavily in the airless chamber, connected umbilically to a huge placenta that provided all the necessary elements for proper growth.

It was Caleb's first entry into a fetus and, while he experienced through the unborn colt's senses a strong feeling of well-being, he missed the tactile, visual and auditory stimuli to which he had become accustomed when entering animals in his usual manner. Yet he felt a strong desire to be on hand at foaling time, to experience from the viewpoint of the colt himself the spasmodic pressures of labor and the ultimate thrust into the outer world, and to share with the colt the drawing in of that first marvelous breath of air. He decided he would ask Doc to let him know when the mare's time was close.

With that thought he returned to himself and continued walking toward the barn. He knew it would probably be at least another hour or so before Judy returned home. She had left early this morning to see some horses that were for sale on a southern Wisconsin farm and planned to be back somewhere between seven and eight this evening. Six o'clock was the barn's regular closing time and the crush of weekend riders and boarders had already dissipated; only three horses were still being ridden in the big ring as Caleb came through the large door at the south end of the building. One of these was his favorite, Button-Eyes, thudding around the ring at a good working trot under Allison Crane. Her posture was straight and true, her back curved slightly inward, with shoulders, hips and feet vertically aligned, her gaze directed straight ahead, her own movements blending smoothly with the gait of the champion horse. As always, Caleb marveled at the sheer magnificence of this animal, at the rippling of his powerful muscles and the proud carriage.

Button-Eyes was one of the few horses at Spring Hill Farm that Caleb enjoyed observing almost as much from his own vantage as from within the animal and he paused to watch now through his own eyes as Allison reined the gelding into a final ten-minute cooling-off walk. As that period ended and she walked the horse into B-Barn to his stall for the final grooming, Caleb walked discreetly behind the horse and rider, watching the way Button-Eyes placed his hooves.

The champion jumper, always one of the most sure-footed animals in the entire barn, momentarily seemed to lose control of his feet, stumbled faintly, staggered slightly in recovery and reestablished his gait. The misstep and recovery were so slight, so vague, so swiftly past, that Allison Crane did not even notice. Had Caleb blinked at that moment, he would have missed it. But he hadn't blinked and now he frowned, never before having observed Button-Eyes as anything other than wholly sure of his footing.

He thought of entering the horse to see if something were wrong but was afraid to do so, knowing that Allison would see him in his dissociated state and problems might ensue. Instead, he lingered close by as she dismounted, removed the saddle and began grooming the animal, currying and brushing and rubbing down. Nothing further in the horse's attitude indicated in any way that there was a problem, yet Caleb felt an uneasiness about the animal he could not comprehend. He determined to remain here until Allison left and then enter the gelding for an interior perspective.

By the time grooming was completed it was after 6:30 P.M. and B-Barn was all but empty of other riders, owners or barn staff. Allison carefully closed and latched the sliding door of the stall, smiled at Caleb and tossed a brief wave in his direction as she headed toward the tack room with her saddle. Caleb waited until she turned out of sight at the far end of B-Barn and then he approached Button-Eyes's stall. He looked inside and saw the big gelding standing quietly, in no apparent discomfort, the stall halter his only accoutrement at the moment.

Caleb was beginning to doubt what he had observed in the aisle. He studied the horse even more closely and suddenly his early concern became underlined as he saw that Button-Eyes's sides were expanding and contracting with his breathing at a rate only minutely faster than normal, but nevertheless faster. It was another manifestation that might easily have passed unnoticed had he not been primed to detect any possible disorder. Without further hesitation, Caleb sent his consciousness into the horse.

Instantly, terrifyingly, he knew *something* was desperately wrong. There was an overwhelming feeling of disorientation, and at the same time an increasing malaise. The breathing was faintly labored and growing more painful, more labored, every second. But the most frightening of all was the disturbing impairment of the animal's vision. Looking through the gelding's eyes at the vertical bars of the door wall facing the outer aisle, Caleb could see that not only was there a ghost image of each of the bars, but that the figure of the boy standing behind the bars was also ghosted. Even as he watched through the horse's dulling vision, the ghost images became stronger, more substantial, losing some of their wraithlike quality. In this brief interval of watching through the host, he saw his own form become identical twins overlaid upon themselves, so that the left eye of one boy became the right eye of the other.

The double-vision shocked him and he turned his concentration inward. He sensed at once a vague imbalance, a positioning of the hooves wider apart than normal as the gelding automatically sought a more solid anchorage, yet with no increased sense of stability. Was this what had instigated that faint stumbling? There was a steady grinding pain in the abdomen which, in practically any other animal, should have predicated convulsive vomiting immediately, but Caleb remembered Doc Patrick telling him early on that horses were incapable of vomiting and therefore such relief for this pain was not possible.

A pervading fear filled Caleb's mind and he transferred back into his own consciousness. The horse was in serious trouble and, though he still had no idea of the nature of the problem, he felt that if he didn't do something immediately, Button-Eyes might become sick enough to die. He stared through the upright bars at the horse and even though the outward manifestations of the animal's growing problem were so slight as to be virtually undetectable to the unalerted eye, he could still strongly sense the seriousness of the malady.

Few people were left in the barn, and no one to whom he could convincingly express the severity of the problem. He *knew* — without knowing how he knew — that something had to be done immediately. There was no way of determining exactly when Judy would be back and it would be a grave error to wait. By going inside the stall and checking Button-Eyes thoroughly close up, he might better be able to ascertain if the problem had external signs that might be a clue to its origin and what he could do to help. Without hesitation he unlatched the stall door, slid it open and stepped inside, reassuring the champion jumper with soft words as he did so.

Button-Eyes was facing the opposite front corner of

the stall from the sliding door and he lifted his head slightly as Caleb entered. His ears came forward momentarily as they often had before when the boy softly chirped or murmured to him. Almost imperceptibly the gelding straightened and, if the stance and breathing before had given some faint clue as to his discomfort, they no longer did so now. It was almost as if the horse were making a conscious effort at bravado, attempting to give the impression that nothing was wrong with him. The big dark eyes seemed clear and alert and the only inconsistency in behavior was that the gelding remained rooted in place. Always before when Caleb had appeared outside the stall, Button-Eyes immediately moved close to have his incredibly soft nostrils rubbed and ears stroked. This time he made no move whatever, not even turning his head to look at the boy, and that alone was highly uncharacteristic.

Caleb knew that other people in the barn had branded Button-Eyes with a slight reputation as a nipper; the horse would accept petting with seeming enjoyment until abruptly he would turn and nip the hand or arm or shoulder of the person doing the stroking. The big horse had never made any attempt to bite Caleb, however, and he did not do so now as the boy's hands reached up, patting his neck and touching the sleek muzzle. But beneath his hands, Caleb could feel the gelding trembling. Moving slowly, he let his hands slide down and onto the chest, across the shoulder, past the swell of the girth and the smooth concavity of the loins to the powerful bulge of hip and haunch.

There was still an uncharacteristic disinclination in the

horse to turn and watch what the boy was doing. Button-Eyes remained motionless, head straight forward, the large eyes unseeingly directed toward the grillwork of the aisle partition of the stall, the hooves firmly planted and tail hanging limply. With one hand resting against the haunch and the other pressed to the loin, Caleb transferred into the animal again and was immediately aghast at how much worse the overall sense of illness was inside. The gelding was hardly aware of the hands of the motionless boy pressed against him. There seemed to be a strong inclination not to move, not to shift the evenly distributed weight to one set of legs or the other, as if to do so would create an uncorrectable imbalance. Breathing was much more difficult now than it had been only a few minutes ago, each expansion of the lungs achieved only with great concentrated effort to force the diaphragm to produce its normal bellows action to inflate and deflate the lungs. An aura of steady pain filled the gelding and Caleb wondered how Button-Eyes could look so normal from the outside and feel so utterly devastated within. In the weeks of working with Doc Patrick, during which he had entered scores of animals with varying degrees of pain from illness or injury, he had never experienced such a terrible feeling. It was then that he realized without any doubt that Button-Eyes was dying. He also knew that sharing the horse's discomfort was accomplishing nothing and once again he transferred back into his own body, not knowing what else to do beyond running to get help.

At that same moment he heard a low exclamation and jerked around to find Judy Boyle standing in the entrance to the stall. Her expression was one of bewilderment and when she spoke her tone of voice was unbelieving, low and controlled.

"Caleb! What do you mean by coming into this stall? I can't believe you'd do it. I'm so disappointed."

"Judy, I —"

"No!" Her hand went up, palm forward, stopping him. "Don't say a word." She sighed and spaced her reiteration: "Not . . . one . . . word! Just walk out of here right now and go out onto the veranda. Wait for me there. I'll be out as soon as I take a look at Button-Eyes."

Again Caleb tried to speak, leaning toward her anxiously, but she shook her head and cut him off, her words still calm but taking on an edge. "I said out — *now!* Do it!"

Caleb turned and walked down the long aisle of B-Barn, his mind in turmoil, the fear of what would happen to him now blending unbearably with the fear of what was affecting Button-Eyes. He stumbled past the lounge and office and out onto the veranda and stood there waiting nervously. Judy's car was parked close by.

In less than five minutes Judy came out. She stopped only a foot or so from the doorway and regarded him with a strange mixture of anger and sorrow. She shook her head. Her voice, now that she was away from the horses and wouldn't alarm them, was more normal in volume, but absolutely cold.

"This is what you do as soon as my back is turned? Oh, Caleb, I expected better things of you. So much better. I never would have believed that you'd break your word to me — that you'd sneak around when you thought I wasn't here and do what you're not allowed to do."

Caleb, humiliated, afraid and angry, finally found his voice. "Judy, Button-Eyes —"

"Be quiet!"

"But Button-Eyes is—"

"I said be quiet, Caleb." Her face was composed and the words more powerful in their lack of heat. "I don't care to hear anything you have to say. Nothing!"

"You don't understand." He was pleading now. *"Listen* to me, Judy, *please!* You've *got* to listen!"

She shook her head and held up her hand again. "Caleb, stop it. I told you, not a word! Just go away. Go on back to the house and stay there. Do not come back to the barn. You are permanently banned from this area. I'll speak to you further when I get home."

She turned to leave, then stopped in the doorway and looked back at him, an enormous sadness in her eyes. "I trusted you," she said. "I believed you were responsible and truthful and honorable. I believed you would live up to your promises, and I warned you what would happen if you broke the rules. You failed me, Caleb; you betrayed my trust. You not only failed me, you also failed your parents. Most of all, you have failed yourself. You're not welcome in the barns anymore." She looked at him steadily for a long moment and then walked into the barn, closing the door quietly behind her.

Caleb stood staring at the door. Numbly, then, he moved toward the fence against which his bicycle leaned, mounted it and pumped with difficulty against the loose, crunchy gravel of the lane to the road. He entered the highway without looking, causing a battered pickup truck to swerve violently to avoid hitting him. He hardly noticed it and paid no attention to the stream of invective the irate driver hurled back at him. He pedaled several hundred yards toward home before looking back toward the Spring Hill barns. The buildings swam in his vision and he blinked.

"I *won't* come back!" he shouted, not caring who heard. "I don't *want* to come back! Button-Eyes is dying and you don't even care. Well, I don't either. You hear me? I don't either!"

There was more he wanted to shout, much more, but suddenly he was crying so hard he couldn't speak.

Chapter 11

IT WAS QUARTER AFTER SEVEN when Caleb entered the house and went directly to the bathroom and washed his face and hands, hardly noting the sting of the cold water. His mind was still in turmoil over what had occurred at the barn and he tried to shove the thoughts away. He dried himself in a daze and abruptly found himself in his room without even knowing how he got there. He didn't know what to do with himself. He turned around three times in place, as if he were lost. Sitting down on the edge of the bed he reached over to the nightstand and picked up the William Beebe book, *Edge of the Jungle*. It had been a gift from Doc Patrick a week ago — an old book that had been his since he was a boy.

Flopping across the spread on his stomach, Caleb started reading where he had left off, but then slammed the book closed after reading the same paragraph three times without comprehension. He got up and went into the family room, turned on the television and flipped disinterestedly from channel to channel. For fifteen minutes he watched an insipid situation comedy before turning off the set and returning to his bedroom. He lay on his back staring unseeingly at the ceiling as the room gradually darkened in the gathering dusk.

He thought about Button-Eyes.

Only the last traces of light still streaked the western horizon when Caleb suddenly leaped up and dashed from the room. He switched on the little brass-shaded lamp on the telephone stand and picked up a slim, shiny black book across the front of which was indented in gold letters *TELEPHONE NUMBERS*. He flipped it open at the tab marked P and immediately found what he was looking for. He lifted the telephone receiver and rapidly punched the numbers. With the receiver at his ear he heard the relays click and the distant buzz of a phone ringing. After the third ring he felt his fears rising that no one was home. But the phone was answered in the midst of the fourth ring.

"Hello?"

"Doc? This is Caleb."

"Ah, Caleb, how are you? You're going with me on rounds in the morning, aren't you?"

The boy didn't reply and in a moment Colin Patrick spoke again, the earlier joviality absent. "What's the matter, son? Are you all right?"

"Yes, I'm . . . all right."

"You don't sound it. What's wrong?"

"Doc . . . Doc . . ." Without warning the heaving sobs came and he had difficulty speaking. "Button-Eyes. It's Button-Eyes. He's . . . Doc, he's . . . he's . . ."

Dr. Patrick's voice was crisp, businesslike, steadying. "Come on, Caleb, settle down now. What's the matter with Button-Eyes?"

"He's dying."

"He's *what?*"

"*Dying!* Button-Eyes is dying. I don't know what's the matter with him, but he's dying!"

"How do you know?"

"I was with him. I saw him, went inside. Doc, he's dying."

"Went inside what? The stall?" He paused. "Or inside him?"

"Both. Allison Crane was riding him in the big ring and I was watching and I thought I saw something wrong and I waited until she left and then I went inside him and there *was* something wrong and then I went inside the stall and then —"

"Whoa! Hold it. Caleb, now listen. Back up and tell me what you saw, what you felt inside the horse, everything. Wait a minute — first of all, did you tell Judy Boyle or anyone else?"

"I tried to tell Judy, but she wouldn't listen. She caught me inside the stall with Button-Eyes. She made me leave the barn and told me not to come back anymore. Doc, she wouldn't listen!"

"Okay, never mind that for now. Did you tell *anyone?*"

"No. Just you. Now."

"How long ago was this?"

"It was about seven, I guess, when Judy made me —"

"No, not that. When was it you first detected something wrong with Button-Eyes?"

"I don't know. Oh, wait! The barn was just closing, so it had to be about six o'clock."

"All right, step by step now, tell me about it. What did you see first that made you think something was wrong?"

"It was when Allison was walking Button-Eyes back to his stall after his cool-off. I was right behind them and he sort of stumbled."

"Stumbled?"

"Well, first he acted like his feet were out of control. Just for a second. Then he sort of stumbled. It wasn't much. Allison didn't even notice."

"Okay, go on. What next?"

"After she rubbed him down and left, I watched him. He looked all right at first and then I saw something was wrong with his breathing." Caleb thought he heard a sharp low exclamation by the vet, but he went on without pause. "He was breathing too fast. Not much, but faster than looked right. That was when I went . . . inside him."

"And?"

"Doc, it was awful! Something awful was wrong. He *hurt* inside — his stomach and his ribs. I never felt anything like that inside any other animal. He was working hard just to make his lungs take in enough air. And he didn't feel right. I don't know how to describe it. He just felt, well, wrong."

"Dizzy?"

"No, not really dizzy, but like . . . like he was apart from himself, and as if . . . I don't know how to describe it . . . but I guess as if his insides were becoming paralyzed."

Doc sucked in a sharp breath and there was tension in his voice when he spoke. "What about stability? Was he weaving?"

"No, not really, but there was something else that scared me."

"What?"

"His eyes. Vision, I mean. He was seeing . . . well, kind of like ghosts." It sounded silly to Caleb now that he had said it aloud and he thought the vet might think him stupid.

"You mean he saw things that weren't there?"

"Not exactly. But the things that were there . . . well, he was seeing whatever they were, but right next to them would be an image of the same thing, only it wasn't solid like the other one; you could see through it."

"Caleb," Doc's voice was gentle, calming, "would it be correct to describe it as a sort of double-vision?"

"Yes. Yes, that's what it was like!"

"And sort of ghostlike — transparent?"

"Yes. At least the first time it was. The second time, a little while later, the second image — the ghost one — was stronger, almost like like there were two of every-thing."

"Wait a minute. You went into Button-Eyes twice? What happened between the first and second time?"

"That's when I went inside the stall. I *had* to! I knew something was wrong, but I wasn't sure yet how bad, or what was making it happen. I got back into myself and then went into the stall and checked him over; rubbed my hands over his head and neck and sides, like you do."

"To what result?"

"I couldn't find anything wrong outside. I mean nothing like an injury or a swelling or anything like that. Button-Eyes didn't even move. Except for raising his head a little and pointing his ears forward for just a second or two. But he didn't turn and look at me, even when I touched him. He just stood there looking straight forward. His breathing didn't seem so bad then, but he just stood there looking straight ahead, as if I weren't even there. He didn't even move his tail. But I could feel him shaking under my hands, you know, trembling. But you couldn't see it."

"That's when you decided he was dying?"

"No, not yet. Not until I went back inside him again, right after that." The memory of it stirred him. "Oh, Doc, I can't tell you how much worse it was, in just that little time. He could only breathe in little shallow breaths and his whole insides hurt. It made me feel like throwing up, just to feel what he was feeling. And I got the feeling that Button-Eyes knew that if he moved or tried to walk, he'd just fall over. That was when the vision was so much more double again, like you were talking about. I think he knows he's dying. I think that's what I felt through him when I was inside, like I knew from what he was feeling that he was just waiting to die."

"What then?"

"That's when Judy came. I was just going from Button-Eyes back into me when she was suddenly there and told me to get out. I tried to tell her about Button-Eyes, but she wouldn't listen. Doc, she's got to listen. She's got to know! Will you call her? Tell her?"

"Caleb, I want you to listen to me now, very carefully.

I don't like what you've described. Not at all." His delivery was more brusque and he went on in a voice filled with a subdued sense of urgency. "From what you've said, there's no time to waste. None. I won't have time to call Judy and go all through this. I'll be out there as soon as I can, but it'll be an hour, anyway. If it's what it sounds like, I'm going to have to detour over to Good Shepherd and pick up something. That'll slow me down, but we can't take the chance of my getting to the barn and then finding I have to go back to the hospital after it anyway. Here's what you do: get over to the barn immediately and talk to Judy. Tell her I'm on my way, but to get Button-Eyes out of his stall right away and outside. He won't want to move, but she should make him go anyway. But slowly. Keep him calm. No noises, no excitement. Keep away from other horses, people, dogs, anything. Keep him away from bright lights. When she gets him outside, she's not to walk him. No sheet or blanket over him, either. She should talk to him quietly, pet him, soothe him, keep him calm. All right, you got that?"

"Yes, but —"

"No buts! Just get back over there and talk to Judy now."

"But she won't lis —" Caleb broke off. Doc had hung up.

Caleb redialed the number to beg Doc to call Judy himself and alert her, but he got a busy signal. With the urgency of the vet's words still filling him, he raced from the house and pedaled back to the barns. The spacious main yard and parking area were barren of people and vehicles. Judy's car was no longer there. It was fully dark now and a warm glow of lights showed here and there from inside the barns, while a single floodlight illuminated the outside front area. Caleb swept up to the barn porch with a scattering of gravel, let his bike drop and thudded across the wooden veranda toward the door.

Inside, all three dogs had heard his approach and were barking wildly and growling. They rushed to the door and Caleb hesitated opening it until they knew it was him. He called to them loudly and heard the timbre of their sounds change to yelps of delight with their recognition of him. Before he could open the door, however, it was thrown wide from the inside by Spring Hill's night guard, Murray Belcher.

"Holly! King! Be quiet! Beau, stop that racket!" The man cupped a hand over his eyes to ward off the floodlight's glare in order to see who was there. His expression turned sour when he saw Caleb.

"Oh, it's you, eh? What're you doing back here?"

"I have to see Judy, Mr. Belcher," Caleb said, breathing heavily from his ride. "It's important!"

Murray was already shaking his head. A truculent, humorless man of about fifty-five, he wore a dirty blue-and-white-striped railroad cap and had a heavy, unkempt gray moustache mottled with tobacco stains. "No way," he said. "Heard about how Miz Judy ordered you out just before I got here. Wish I'd'a been here t'see it."

"Please, Mr. Belcher. I *have* to see Judy right away."

"Ain't here. Left to go into town about an hour ago. You can be glad she ain't here. She'd chew you up in little pieces if she was. She give everybody orders you wasn't allowed t'step foot in the barns no more. So you better git, boy."

Caleb shook his head in anguish. "You don't understand. It's Button-Eyes. He's sick. Doc Patrick's coming to help and we have to take care of him right away."

"Just what're you trying to pull, boy?" Murray growled, suspicious now. "Not twenty minutes ago I was looking right in at Button-Eyes and he was standing there just like always. I don't know what you're up to, but I heard about people kicked off horse farms coming back at night to burn the barns down. You just get t'hell off this property right now. Let me see you 'round here one more time and I'll set your fanny on fire with a load of birdshot. Now git!"

"But Doc told me —"

"I said *git!*" He took a menacing step toward Caleb and the boy backed away and then ran to his bicycle. The three dogs, evidently considering this break in the regularity of their existence an event worth celebrating, cavorted around the bicycle barking loudly until he reached the highway. Only at sharp commands from Murray did they give up and trot back to the barn with tails waving jauntily.

Caleb pedaled rapidly a hundred yards or so and then stopped. Doc's instructions for Judy weighed heavily in him and he didn't know what to do. He disliked and feared Murray Belcher and took seriously his threat concerning the birdshot. He considered pedaling into Algonquin and trying to locate Judy, but rejected the idea immediately. It would take too much time, and supposing he couldn't even find her? He weighed the idea of merely waiting in the darkness here until Doc's white van showed up and then following him to the barn. No, that wouldn't do, either. An hour or more might be wasted just waiting and there was no time to lose. That's what Doc had said.

He knew what he had to do. Stepping off his bike, he wheeled it off the road and down into the ditch where he laid it on its side in the grass, hidden from any passing headlights. Then he climbed the fence and slipped silently through the darkened pasture toward the back of the barn. Circling widely, his heart hammering in his chest, he came to the sliding back door of B-Barn, close to Button-Eyes's stall. A single bare hundred-watt bulb burned above the door. Gripping the edge of the big metal barrier, he tried to move it and couldn't. Putting his shoulder to it and trying again, he strained hard and abruptly the door slid open about five feet with a faint rasp of the metal rollers on their track.

Caleb waited outside a moment, staring in through the opening, seeing the long, deserted aisle of B-Barn stretching out before him as if it were something from a dream. He half expected to see one or more of the dogs come bounding around the corner at the far end, alerted by the sound the door had made, but there was nothing. At length he slipped inside and crept swiftly to Button-Eyes's stall. As was common practice at night, only half the usual number of fluorescents were burning in the barn, but they shed sufficient light to see into the stalls.

Button-Eyes was standing as Murray had said he was, though not in exactly the same position in which Caleb had last seen him. He had moved closer to the partition between his stall and the next and was facing the door. To the casual glance, nothing at all seemed wrong. Caleb's inspection, however, was not casual; and to him two alarming things were immediately apparent. First there was the horse's breathing: shallow, harsh, pained — not so much a gasping as it was a great effort merely to inhale. Caleb had not previously heard a horse breathing like that and it frightened him. The second thing was the gelding's posture: While indeed he was standing, he was actually leaning heavily against the partition wall, most of his weight propped on the outer legs.

For just a moment Caleb entered the animal and was appalled at the overwhelming sense of *wrongness* being experienced. The entire body cavity hurt — not with a dull pervading ache, but rather with excruciating pain that seemed to emanate from every cell simultaneously. The horse's eyes were open, staring unseeingly toward the front of the stall, and by this time the double-vision was so pronounced that for Caleb it took on the aspect of a mirror image, one beside the other, creating a strong sense of vertigo. Worst of all was the incredible difficulty in breathing; at no time could an adequate amount of air be drawn into the lungs and the front quarters of the body cavity writhed in a vain effort to suck in a sufficient volume. The discomfort was so severe that Caleb couldn't bear to remain in the gelding any longer and transferred back into his own consciousness, feeling weak and fearful from the experience.

A low, brief, practically inaudible groan escaped the horse and, without further hesitation, Caleb opened the stall door, ignoring both the rasp of metal against metal as he slid the principal bolt, and the grating sound — loud in the stillness of the barn — of the heavy door sliding open on its rollers. He moved inside and stopped next to the horse, his hands immediately rubbing Button-

Eyes's neck and shoulder in a comforting manner. The gelding appeared not even to notice and Caleb's fears increased.

He leaned his forehead against the muscular shoulder, thinking, trying to remember all that Doc had instructed him to tell Judy to do for the horse before he got there. No noise, he had said, and no excitement. Keep him away from people and dogs and other horses. Get him out from under the lights. That was it — the first admonition: Get him outside right away.

Caleb gripped the halter and tried to lead Button-Eyes from the stall, but all he succeeded in doing was slightly turning the horse's head and causing the neck to stretch out a bit. He tugged harder on the halter but with no more effect than if the device had been attached to a huge boulder. Button-Eyes's left side was still resting solidly against the stall's partition, his rib cage heaving, head lowered and ears drooping. Moving around behind, petting the horse, stroking him, talking softly all the while, Caleb placed his shoulder against the rump, braced himself and shoved. Except for a vague swaying, the horse did not move.

"Walk, Button-Eyes!" he grunted. "Please, walk! I've got to get you outside. Come on. *Come on!*"

Still there was no response and Caleb became aware that other horses in nearby stalls were becoming alarmed. One spooked and slammed into the side of its stall and another kicked the wall with a resounding crash. Two or three snorted and one began a harsh whinnying which broke off abruptly. Then the dogs were at the open stall door, King and Beau barking frantically and Holly, hackles raised, snarling.

"King! Beau! Stop it! Stop barking!" The boy's words hissed out of him and, recognizing his voice and scent, the dogs relaxed and Beau's tail curved up and waved happily from side to side. They stood at the stall door, the three canines, confused by what was going on and unsure of their own roles in the matter.

"What in the *hell* are you doing, boy?" The loud nasal twang of Murray Belcher filled the barn. At his angered tone, the dogs resumed their growling, looking from the night guard to the boy. Murray stood in the aisle behind them, his left fist clenched and an old headless ax handle gripped threateningly in his right hand.

Oddly, Caleb no longer felt fear, only a desperate urgency, and he stepped a pace away from the gelding. "Mr. Belcher, listen to me! Button-Eyes is dying. I don't know what's the matter with him, but he's *dying!* Get Judy. Please, get Judy! We've got to help him."

Murray Belcher was an irascible man, but he was no fool. For the first time he shifted his glare away from the boy and looked at the champion jumper. His mouth dropped open. The abject misery of the horse was instantly apparent and now it was Belcher who stood uncertainly.

"Please, Mr. Belcher," Caleb continued. "Doc is on his way, but you've got to get Judy here to help. Don't you understand? I'm telling you the truth. Button-Eyes is going to die if we don't help him."

The night guard's prominent Adam's apple bobbed and he jerked his head once. "I think I know where I kin reach her," he said. He whirled around and the makeshift club was still gripped in his hand as he clumped at a heavy run back down the aisle toward the office. King, barking again, raced after him and, after only a moment's hesitation, Holly and Beau followed.

The disturbance, especially the barking of the dogs, had the effect of rousing Button-Eyes from his lethargy. The gelding straightened, groaning at the effort, and the shallow breaths wheezed more agonizingly in his nostrils. His head lifted slightly and Caleb transferred his consciousness back into him. The pain was markedly worse, but greater awareness had returned and the horse was more sensitive both to the still form of the boy beside him and to the pain throbbing within him. The chest heaved violently to activate the diaphragm so the lungs could inhale a great swell of air, but still the breathing continued dangerously shallow and rapid.

With all his concentration, Caleb willed the animal to move, the tendrils of his mind reaching out desperately in the effort to force Button-Eyes to walk, striving to make the muscles of the legs function. Nothing. As always, Caleb was only an observer without the slightest control or motivation possible over his host. Mentally moaning in his anxiety, the boy returned to himself, moved immediately to the horse's head and gripped the halter. He stroked the gelding's muzzle with one hand and pulled steadily on the halter with the other, all the while talking softly, soothingly, coaxingly.

"Come on, Button-Eyes, come on. That's a good boy. You're alert now. Come on, come with me outside. Please, Button-Eyes, *please*, come with me."

The horse's neck stretched out with the pressure of Caleb's pull, but still he balked. Then the right front hoof stepped out, only a little, a few inches, and the left rear

moved up the same distance to compensate. A movement
of the legs had started and the left front and right rear
came forward in the same way. With the motion begun, it
continued mechanically and Caleb exulted inwardly, increasing his quiet urgings while maintaining steady pressure.

Button-Eyes walked.

It was, at best, an uncoordinated, staggering gait, short-
paced and unsure, evidently painful if the gelding's increased grunting were an indication, but Button-Eyes was
walking nonetheless. Head down, ears and tail limp, he
stepped to the urgings of the boy, following him slowly
out of the stall and into the aisle, turning trancelike in the
direction Caleb turned him, moving painfully, blunder-
ingly, but steadily toward the partially opened door.

Caleb shoved the huge door wider as he reached it and
step by step led the jumper outside into the night. The air
was cool, crisp, with the touch of approaching autumn. A
gentle breeze was stirring where before there had been
none. The freshness of the air had an immediate effect on
the gelding. His actions became less mechanical, more
controlled, though the imbalanced, uncoordinated gait
continued. The large head came up somewhat and, though
his gasping for air did not cease, there was a subtle
change, as if this air were better for him than the warmer,
heavier air inside the barn.

By the light of the single bare bulb over the door, Caleb
led him until they were about thirty feet from the door
and close to the rails of the back paddock. Here Caleb
stopped. Without the continuing pressure on the halter,
Button-Eyes stopped as well. The big horse swayed and

nearly fell to one side, but caught himself with an effort and stood with all four hooves planted abnormally apart, legs stiffened against a threatened buckling of the knees. Following the vet's instructions, Caleb continued to pet the horse and speak quietly to him for the next ten minutes.

"Caleb! What is all this?" Judy Boyle strode swiftly toward him from the B-Barn door, the dogs clustered at her feet and Murray Belcher bringing up the rear.

"Get them away, Judy." Caleb spoke softly but with intensity, pointing with his free hand toward the dogs. "Doc said to keep them away. Please! Doc'll be here soon."

Judy stopped, frowning, opened her mouth to reply and then closed it without doing so. She turned and looked at the night guard who had stopped behind her. "Murray," she said in a low voice, "take the dogs back inside and close the door. Go up front and wait for Doc Patrick to arrive and have him get back here with us as soon as he comes."

Murray bobbed his head and chirped to the dogs. They followed, but only reluctantly, their attitudes clearly expressing disappointment. Ignoring their departure, Judy turned back to Caleb and Button-Eyes. As she looked at the horse more closely, she paled. The quasi-alertness that had returned to the gelding had vanished and he had reverted to looking fully as bad as when he had been in the stall, the impression intensified by his present ungainly, propped posture on straddled legs. The gelding's breathing remained badly labored, accompanied by an ominous whistling sound at each short exhalation from the open mouth. A barely perceptible shuddering swept the animal.

"We've got to get a blanket over him," she said, starting to turn away.

"No!" Caleb's response halted her. "Doc said nothing over him. No blanket, no sheet, nothing. And he's not supposed to walk any more. We have to keep him quiet and calm."

She nodded and returned to stand near the boy, placing her hands on the horse and rubbing him, talking softly to him. The familiar voice and touch seemed to help and the trembling eased, though the gasping did not. Without altering her soothing tone or ceasing the stroking, Judy looked at Caleb, who was still gripping the halter.

"When did you talk to Doc?"

"At home. On the phone. Just before I came back."

"What did he say was wrong with him?" She tilted her head toward the horse.

Caleb shrugged. "He didn't. Just told me what to tell you to do until he got here. You weren't here, so I did what he said. He told me he'd be at least an hour getting here."

"Why so long?"

"Because he had to stop first at Good Shepherd Hospital."

"Good Shepherd? In Barrington? What in heaven's name for?"

Another shrug. "I don't know. He just said he couldn't take the chance of getting here and then finding he had to go back to the hospital after it anyway."

"After *it?*" Judy looked confused. "After what?"

"I don't know. He didn't say and there wasn't time to talk."

Judy shook her head, unable to understand how this

had all come about. Caleb thought she would ask him more questions, but now she fell silent, evidently preferring to wait for Doc's arrival. Though their conversation had ceased, both continued to sooth the gelding, rubbing and crooning.

Dr. Colin Patrick arrived a quarter-hour later, carrying his big satchel in one hand and a small box in the other. Neither Murray nor the dogs were with him. He looked a little haggard, perhaps from his recent illness, and, except for a grunt and nod, he paid no attention to the boy or the woman, his concentration on the horse. The illumination from the bulb over the door was minimal, but enough to work by. Placing the satchel and box on the ground, the vet inspected Button-Eyes swiftly but thoroughly, noting immediately the stance, labored breathing and drooping posture. Removing a large thermometer from a case within the satchel, he took the horse's temperature rectally, reading the figures under the beam of a penlight flashlight he extracted from his breast pocket. He was scowling as he put the thermometer away.

"No appreciable fever," he muttered. He then used the penlight to look briefly into the horse's eyes, after which he leaned his head against the heaving chest to listen. He glanced at Judy. "Good thing you got him outside in the fresher air when you did. How'd you manage it?"

Judy's reply was terse. "I didn't. I only got here a short while ago. Caleb brought him out."

The vet shot a glance at Caleb from beneath the shaggy brows and made an approving murmur. He squatted beside the bag and box, speaking softly to Judy as he did so. "I have to tell you, it's bad. This animal's in *extremis*. We may not be able to save him. We'll try."

"Doc, for God's sake, *what is wrong?*" Her voice had become sharp with anxiety and the vet immediately shook his head in warning.

"Easy. Speak quietly if you have anything to say. No loud noises. No disturbance."

Judy was not to be put off and repeated herself, softly but demandingly. "What's wrong?"

Doc Patrick pursed his lips. "I'm not positive. I think I know, but I could be wrong. If I am, he's dead. But he's dead anyway if we don't do something fast."

"Well, do whatever you have to do but, Doc, will you please answer the question!" The words hissed out past clenched teeth. "What . . . is . . . wrong?"

The veterinarian had removed a large standard hypodermic syringe from the satchel and was opening the small box. He took a deep breath. "I've never treated it before. Never even encountered it before, but it's in the literature and it all fits. It's botulism."

"*Botulism!*" She was incredulous. "In a horse?"

Doc Patrick removed a short squat bottle of serum packed in ice within the box, held it upside down and pushed the needle through the red rubber seal. "I don't know what else it could be."

"But . . . *how?*"

Doc glared. "I don't know. We'll find out later. Just forget the questions until I administer this antitoxin. Go get me a clean basin. Better yet, make it a clean gallon jug, if you've got one."

Judy Boyle hesitated, then walked swiftly into the barn. Doc continued with his preparations, drawing two-thirds of the transparent, faintly yellowish serum from the bottle into the syringe. Without wasted movements he replaced the serum bottle in the box and squirted a tiny jet of the fluid straight up to expel any air. Back at the satchel he removed an alcohol-saturated cotton swab from a jar and moved to the gelding's head. Maintaining his grip on the halter, Caleb stepped out of the way as much as possible and watched with fearful fascination as Doc located the jugular in the horse's neck just behind the jawline, rubbed the skin with the swab and then deftly plunged the needle into the thick blood vessel. There was no reaction from Button-Eyes and as soon as the plunger was fully depressed and the needle jerked out, Doc swabbed the spot again and dropped the cotton.

Returning to the satchel, the vet put away the hypodermic syringe and took out four narrow-necked pint bottles. All were the same size and shape, three with yellow-sealed caps and the fourth blue. Consecutively he broke the seals with his thumbnail, stripped off the plastic material and set them on the ground. Then he removed another syringe — this one very large — from the satchel. He muttered something under his breath and glanced up. His words were edged with irritation.

"Where's that —" He broke off as he saw Judy striding from the barn toward them, a translucent gallon jug locked on her index finger. "Oh, there she is. Give it to me, please." He held out his hand toward her.

Without speaking, Judy handed him the container and watched closely as he set the oversized syringe down across the top of the satchel and, in succession, emptied the four pint bottles into the jug. He capped the large container firmly and then swirled it without hard shaking, mixing the fluids but avoiding the formation of air bubbles. When finished, he exhaled deeply.

"Okay, that's done." He glanced at the owner. "Judy, this is a three-to-one mixture — one part fifty percent dextrose to three parts Ringer's Solution."

Judy nodded in understanding, but Caleb couldn't help blurting, "What's Ringer's Solution?"

Doc shifted his gaze to the boy as he gave Judy the jug to hold at an angle while he filled the large syringe. "Ringer's is a saline solution with minerals — calcium, magnesium, elements of blood — injected intravenously. Button-Eyes needs fluids and strength. Energy from the dextrose. This'll give it to him."

Disinfecting the skin in a new place, he injected the full contents of the syringe and turned back to Judy to refill it. Dose after dose followed the first until the jug was nearly empty. As he bent to replace the instrument in his satchel, he looked at Judy.

"All right, thanks. Now you go get your night man and bring him back here — without the dogs! — to stay with Button-Eyes. Then you and I have some investigating to do. We're also going to have to check out every horse in the barn, you know that."

Judy murmured a gloomy assent and walked off. Colin Patrick straightened up his equipment and snapped the satchel closed. He looked around and saw Judy was no longer in sight and turned back to Caleb.

"Okay, you and I are going to have to determine whether that helped Button-Eyes or if it's going to kill him." He took the halter from Caleb's grasp. "I want you to go inside him like you do. Just briefly. Sense what you can and then come back out and tell me about it."

The boy smiled, but the expression faded and he became slack-jawed as he transferred into Button-Eyes. The pain was still there, filling the animal and instilling a new wave of fear in Caleb. But then he noted that in the gelding's pain there was a difference now. While still strong, it was not so all-pervasive as before, and the labor of breathing had eased appreciably. The double-vision was still occurring, but the second image was no longer one of mirror clarity; it was more transparent and evidently fading. A sense of renewed strength, engendered by the Ringer's Solution and dextrose mixture, was flooding through Button-Eyes and while he had not changed his stance, Caleb could feel the muscles tensing as if in preparation for just that. Even during the half-minute he was inside, the horse raised his head and his ears became more expressive. Returning to himself, Caleb looked at Doc and smiled, more broadly this time.

"He's better. He still hurts inside, but he's getting better all the time. The double-vision's fading, too." Caleb went on, recounting the impressions he had assimilated within the horse. When the boy finished, the vet squeezed his shoulder and matched his smile. "Good boy. That's a —"

He broke off as Judy and Murray emerged from the barn and stopped next to them. He told Judy he thought Button-Eyes would live and chuckled at the relief she expressed. Handing the halter to Murray, he gave the man instructions to keep the horse still and calm, to pet and vocally soothe him until receiving further instructions. After that the three of them — the vet, the owner and the boy — walked toward the barn.

"Judy," Doc said, "I'm sorry it took me so long to get here. I can't keep botulism antitoxin on hand and normally to get it, if I thought I might have a need, I'd have to order it from Atlanta. No good in this case. It would have to have been flown here and even with emergency priority, it would've arrived too late. Botulism causes death in thirty-six hours from ingestion, with medical aid futile after twelve to eighteen hours. I don't know how long ago Button-Eyes ingested the toxin, but I do know we caught it just in time. Anyway, there was no time to get it from Atlanta and the only other hope was that Good Shepherd had some on hand for emergencies. Same antitoxin for humans and animals, so no problem there. I called them as soon as I finished speaking with Caleb and, fortunately, they had a small supply. I can't say they were any too happy about dispensing some of it to a horse doctor." He chuckled again. "Lost ten minutes just convincing them."

"I still don't understand how a horse could get botulism," Judy said. She was the first to step inside the barn, followed by Doc and then Caleb. "Most of all, I don't understand for a minute how you even came to suspect that Button-Eyes had it."

They stopped before the open door to Button-Eyes's stall and Doc inclined his head toward Caleb. "You can thank your young friend here. He detected something wrong with the horse and that's when he went into the stall, where you nabbed him and tossed him out on his ear — or whatever you tossed him out on." He laughed. "Justifiably, I might add. I would've done the same under similar conditions. But it was a good thing he took the initiative. After he got home and stewed about it for a while, he called me. I pried the symptoms out of him and about halfway through began to suspect botulism. No time wasted after that."

"But how could Caleb have known the symptoms?" Judy persisted.

"Later," Doc said. "First things first. Caleb, it's pushing eleven o'clock and that's pretty late for you. Better go on home and come back in the morning. I'll still be here. There's a lot of work to do. We won't be going on rounds until this problem is settled. I'll see you then."

Caleb nodded, reluctant to go but suddenly very tired.

"There's some potato salad and cold cuts in the refrigerator," Judy said. "Milk, too. Go ahead and eat. You must be starved. I don't know when I'll get home. Or even *if* I will tonight."

The boy smiled and nodded again. He set off down the aisle, speaking over his shoulder. "See you in the morning, Doc. Good night, Judy."

"Good night, Caleb." She hesitated and then spoke again, stopping him. "Caleb. I . . . want to thank you. And I want to apologize for what happened earlier in the evening. I'm sorry. I didn't know."

Caleb grinned, waved and started walking again. The pleasant smell of ring dirt and leather, horses and hay filled his nostrils and he felt very good.

Chapter 12

WHEN HE RETURNED to Spring Hill in the morning, Caleb found Dr. Colin Patrick and Judy Boyle still carefully checking the other horses. Both of them were showing the strain of working all night and, though an hour or more of labor still faced them, Doc agreed without much persuading to stop for a break. In the office they had hot coffee and doughnuts, the latter brought in by one of the staff, and while they relaxed they filled Caleb in on what had happened during the night after his departure.

Most important, Button-Eyes was clearly out of danger. Not well, by any means, nor would he be for a day or two, but certainly he was past the crisis and improving hourly. In the small hours of the morning, Doc had given him another injection of the antitoxin — considerably smaller this time — and what remained of the dextrose and Ringer's Solution mixture.

The first matter of consequence had been to determine the source of the botulism. It had not been especially difficult to trace the cause. They discovered that during the forenoon of the preceding day a new load of baled hay, originating from downstate Illinois, had been delivered by a supplier. Shortly afterward, some of the bales had been loaded aboard a flatbed wagon and pulled by tractor down the aisles until the full load had been distributed. Then two of the barn hands had moved down the aisles, breaking the bales apart and tossing the proper amount onto the floor of each stall. Button-Eye's stall, being the outermost in B-Barn, was the final one supplied in that feeding. A new bale had been broken apart at that point and the gelding's portion tossed in.

Upon inspecting the stall, Doc and Judy had found some of the uneaten residue of that hay against the back wall. Doc had picked it up and, though there was nothing visibly wrong with it, when he held it to his nose he detected a faint but unmistakable odor of animal decay. They located the remainder of that bale still on the wagon and carefully dissected it. A few inches from where it had been broken to give Button-Eyes his share, they discovered the desiccated remains of a rat. The rodent had evidently been killed by the mower when the hay was cut, raked into a windrow with it and subsequently encased during the baling operation.

The remains were withered and dry and the vet's opinion was that the rat had been dead about six weeks. Doc concluded that it had rotted within the bale and its juices during this time had seeped into much of that hay. Had Button-Eyes attempted to eat any portion of the hay with the actual physical remains of the rat still in it, the taste would probably have turned him away. But the portion he ate had been only lightly coated with the fluids of the disintegrating rat, and those fluids had eventually dried. Doc's opinion was that Button-Eyes had probably not enjoyed the hay, but that the taste had not been bad enough for him to reject it. Nonetheless, the bacterium *Clostridium botulinum*, which forms the toxin called botulin, though dormant in the dried juices, was viable. Upon being ingested by the gelding, it had swiftly become active as the deadly disease. The clue that had first alerted Colin Patrick to the possibility of botulism was the sense of internal incapacitation Caleb had described. Botulism attacks the nervous system and the growing paralysis of the diaphragm causes the shortness of breath. If not checked in its onslaught, within thirty-six hours — and occasionally in as short a time as eighteen hours — the diaphragm would be paralyzed to such an extent that death by suffocation would result. The double-vision and uncoordinated movements of the horse were supportive symptoms.

The possibility, however remote, that other bales of the new shipment of hay might have been similarly affected had galvanized Judy to action. She had called in several barn hands in the middle of the night and all the remaining bales were taken far out into the back lot where they were at this time being burned. Following the removal of the bales, all the stalls into which hay from that shipment had been tossed were thoroughly checked and every remaining scrap collected, also for burning.

While those efforts were going on, Doc and Judy had plunged into the work of examining every horse, whether or not it had received any of the new hay. This entailed making each of the animals walk to test coordination and balance, listening to its respiration and performing several other tests. All of the horses in B-Barn had been checked first, but none had shown any symptoms of the disease. That was encouraging, but the examinations would still go on until each had been given a clean bill of health. At this point, however, Doc expected to find no other infected animals.

"What I don't yet fully comprehend," said Judy, finishing the last of her coffee and looking speculatively at Caleb, "is how you were able to describe Button-Eyes's symptoms to Doc over the phone so accurately that he was able to diagnose the problem as botulism."

Caleb felt a faint flush creeping up his neck and, at the same time, a return of the old fear that his *in*-sight talent would be disclosed and again create difficulties. He shot a glance at the veterinarian. Doc returned the barest suggestion of a shake of his head before setting down his cup and rising.

"Hate to ring down the curtain on this pleasant respite," he said, "but we can talk later on. Judy, let's get the rest of this job done before we both collapse. You want to come along, Caleb?"

Earlier, Caleb had fully anticipated that he would accompany them as they resumed their examination of the horses. Now, in light of the uncomfortable probing by Judy, he decided against it, reluctant to give her the opportunity to ask questions he did not want to answer. He harbored a faint hope that if he could forestall them, she might not get back to the subject again so pertinently in that direction.

"I think I'll go outside to the big exercise lot and watch whatever horses are being worked."

"Okay." It was Judy who replied, finding nothing unusual in the boy's preference. "We'll see you later. Come on, Doc."

She stepped through the doorway, but Doc hesitated before leaving. He put his arm around Caleb and gave him an affectionate hug. "Don't worry," he said, keeping his voice low, "we'll get around it. It's still our secret." At Caleb's relieved smile he looked at the boy with a warm, approving gaze. "I'm very proud of what you did, Caleb. More than I can really tell you. We've got a lot in store for us. Together. That's a promise."

Then he was gone and Caleb sauntered out of the barn toward the big exercising and practice jumping compound adjacent to Pyott Road — the same lot in which he had seen the horses on that first day when his parents had driven him here. The sun was bright this morning and the air crisp with the promise it had held last night of approaching autumn.

Caleb walked slowly, thinking about all that had occurred. The final words of Colin Patrick had stirred him to think with more than idle curiosity about where his future lay from here. The prospect of continuing to work with Doc Patrick and then eventually going on to become a veterinarian in his own right was, in many respects, appealing. Caleb had no doubt now that the talent he possessed could make him perhaps the most outstanding veterinarian of all time. The idea of helping sick and injured animals was not unattractive. If he didn't do that, what else could he do with his ability?

And yet . . .

Something about the whole prospect was not quite right and his brow knitted as he walked toward the outside lot, wondering why he was not wholly overjoyed with the possibilities that working with Doc could open for him. What more could he expect? What else could he do? What was it, if anything, that appealed to him more?

He reached the board fence of the big outdoor ring and watched with casual interest as two horses, Royal Flush and Gay Blade, were put through their paces. Owned by the barn, the seven-year-old Royal Flush was a beautiful thoroughbred, powerfully muscled and a deep shiny black, which was the basis for his name. One of Spring Hill's champion hunters, he was being exercised by his handler, Jane Gebhardt. Caleb's eyes lighted as he watched the proud gait of the gelding. The horse's ears were upright, his dark eyes keenly alert, neck outstretched, impeccable tail flowing behind with silken waves of light flashing down its length at the tempo of the horse's perfect trot.

The other horse, Gay Blade, was an Anglo-Arab — half thoroughbred and half Arabian. A nine-year-old dapple-gray, he was being ridden by one of the newer girl students at the barn, Frances Donovan. A freckled, titian-haired, rather plain girl of fourteen, she was walking him slowly along the fence, an indication that she had completed her morning lessons and was now cooling him off.

Because the top rail of the fence was directly in his line of vision, Caleb stooped and slipped through, then squatted on his heels with his lower back comfortably braced against the bottom rail. His eyes were on Royal Flush as Jane competently put him through a series of smooth figure-eights in the center of the ring. Without even thinking about it, Caleb let his consciousness flow into the black gelding and immediately felt a lift of his spirits at the controlled balance of grace and power in the animal. The flawless raising and lowering of his hooves, the jauntiness of his carriage and attitude, the harmony between horse and rider, all these were a fluid poetry of motion and Caleb exulted in sharing the sensations.

Returning to himself, he smiled wryly, realizing that the final question he had asked himself only a few moments ago was now answered. What appealed to him more than anything else was simply transferring himself into other creatures and experiencing through them the infinite realm of possible sensations. Not just in horses, but in *anything* living.

Becoming a doctor of veterinary medicine might be a gratifying profession, a way to do something worthwhile and earn a good livelihood, but what satisfactions did it hold that could possibly compare with the exhilaration of soaring on motionless wings with a hawk high over forest or meadow? What could compare with plunging along inside a rabbit running at full speed through the windings of an all-but-invisible trail in deep grasses? What might possibly rank with the delectability of sharing with a butterfly the delights of visiting one fragrant flower after another in a rewarding quest for nectar?

As a veterinarian, his future could have many rewards, but he was certain that in such a profession — or in any other human endeavor, for that matter — such rewards would be distinctly limited compared to those he could experience in the world of nature. The drinking in of golden sunshine on his own lush leaves; the excitement of surging through crystalline waters of lake or stream in the consciousness of a fish; the thrill of feeling a spring peeper's lusty cries bursting forth from the bulging throat sac he shared; the incredible drama of the stalk as he occupied the consciousness of a weasel intent upon a chipmunk; the list was glorious, incomparable . . . and endless.

That was what he wanted — that, more than anything else he knew or ever could know of his own experience. His smile faded as he descended to the reality of the here and now. And how, he asked himself, could he exist in such a way? How could he support himself? How could he live the sort of life he was expected to live if he were always fearful that his secret talent would be exposed, that he would be held up to scorn and ridicule? He shook his head, the old depression returning at the insolubility of his problem, the awful incongruity of his whole existence.

A dozen yards away to his right, Frances Donovan was still walking her gelding along the fence, now coming directly toward him. He turned and faced in that direction and, as easily as he had slipped into the consciousness of Royal Flush, so now he did the same with Gay Blade.

Ahead, with the dapple-gray's vision, he could see himself hunkered against the fence, sightlessly watching this approach. Gay Blade was a steady, quiet horse, which made him a favorite of such students as the Donovan girl: students newly learning the fundamentals of good equestrian form. Unlike a fair number of the barn's horses, Gay Blade never took advantage of an inexperienced rider, never tried to scrape the rider off his back against a fence or wall, or went into a fit of bucking or other such show of temperament to satisfy himself. He was not a classy mount and certainly would never win any kind of prize. He was simply one of the more reliable school horses at Spring Hill Farm, upon whose back scores of new riders had been indoctrinated to the world of equitation. As such, he held a place of affection in the hearts of many.

Gay Blade was still breathing a little heavily at the paces Frances Donovan had put him through over the past hour. Though cooling down at the present walking gait to which she held him, the gelding was still in high spirits. He tossed his head and nickered as he neared the form of the boy. Frances herself, cheeks flushed and eyes bright, smiled down at the squatting boy as Gay Blade automatically moved out from the fence a bit to pass him closely on the left.

"Good morning, Caleb." Her voice was as bright and cheerful as the new day. "Isn't it a great morning?"

The boy made no move and didn't turn his head to look at her. Even when the horse passed out of his line of vision, he still didn't move and seemed to be staring at something in the distance. Frances reined in, stopping Gay Blade only a foot or so past him. She swiveled around in her saddle to see what it was he appeared to be so intent upon. Generally in that direction, a large column of blue-white smoke was rising nearly straight up, far off in the back lot, and the girl nodded to herself.

"That's where they're burning the poisoned hay," she told him. "You heard about that, didn't you?"

Inside Gay Blade, Caleb heard her words and thought that he probably should transfer out of the patiently standing gelding and back into his own consciousness. At that precise moment, an insect alighted upon the dapple-gray's left rear leg, just above the hock. The tickling sensation as it landed and then walked a few steps caused an immediate reaction. Gay Blade's tail flicked and a cluster of stuck-together hairs slammed across the insect's body. To the half-inch-long yellow jacket, it was a punishing blow. Just as the horse's reaction had been immediate and automatic, so was the wasp's. She arched her body and drove the long hollow stiletto that was her stinger deep into the gelding's flesh. The simultaneous tightening of her abdominal muscles compressed a tiny bulb at the base of her stinger, sending a charge of highly virulent venom surging through the needlelike tube. The powerful poison, invading the tissues of the gelding's flesh, created an instantaneous burst of searing pain. The chain of events, occurring with split-second rapidity, resulted in a third and final automatic reaction: Gay Blade gave a sharp snort and his left rear hoof shot up and back in a powerful kick which, in a stall, would easily have splintered the pine paneling.

The hoof slammed into the back of the squatting boy's head with incredible force, sending him into a limp, face-down sprawl in the dirt, his limbs askew, as if he were a rag doll carelessly thrown aside. Within the gelding, Caleb felt the jolt through the leg as the hoof connected with flesh and bone with crushing impact. The burning of the wasp sting just over the hock was severe and Caleb shared it with the horse. Through the ears of his host he heard the piercing, terror-filled scream of his rider and felt Gay Blade shy violently.

Frances Donovan was pitched onto the ground in a heap. Unhurt, but still gripped with horror and shock, she scrambled on all fours to the motionless figure of the boy as Gay Blade pranced away from them.

In the center of the ring, Royal Flush reared high, alarmed at the scream from the Donovan girl and at the unusual actions of Gay Blade. Had Jane Gebhardt been less skilled in riding, she would almost certainly have been thrown, but she clung to the hunter's back until he settled and then leaped down and raced toward the crawling girl and prone boy.

The whole sequence of events had been compressed in a phenomenally brief time span. Even as Gay Blade continued to shy and prance, even as Frances scrambled across the ground toward the motionless boy, even as the riderless Royal Flush trotted nervously toward the far fence and Jane Gebhardt ran toward the two youngsters, Caleb attempted to transfer his consciousness back into his own body.

He could not.

With mounting panic, he concentrated more, strove to force himself into the flaccid figure, to regain occupation of his corporeal self. The effort had less effect than if he had attempted to transfer himself into a rock or a fencepost.

Frances had by this time reached the boy's inert form and she touched the back of his head. It was a spongy, blood-soaked mass and beneath her fingers she could feel the splinters of crushed bone grating together. Before Jane could reach her, Frances went into hysterics, screaming uncontrollably, her eyes rolling wildly, the freckles standing out like brown paint flecks against a face suddenly gone the color of new putty.

Jane rushed up and flung herself down on her knees, taking in at a glance the appalling injury to the boy's head, feeling the gorge rising in her throat and holding down the nausea by great effort of will. She snatched the screaming girl by the shoulders and shook her savagely.

"Stop it, Franny, *stop it!*"

The screaming continued. Jane released her hold and swept out a hand in a brief arc, smacking the girl's cheek with stinging shock. The shrieking cut off so suddenly it was as if a switch had been thrown. For an instant the wide blue eyes stared uncomprehendingly at the handler and then recognition returned and she looked again at the boy. A spreading patch of blood was turning the soil into reddish mud and the girl's eyes rolled up in her head. She sagged limply to the ground.

The scream of pure terror has a quality all its own, apart from any other human sound. It strikes an atavistic reaction in all who hear it. The penetrating, far-carrying screams of Frances Donovan had split the quiet morning air. Inside the barn, horses stamped and snorted and already people had dropped what they were doing and were converging at a run from all directions. Handlers, boarders, barn hands, instructors and students erupted from every doorway, including the main office entry. A sports car that had just pulled into the lane slammed to a stop and disgorged two young women in riding clothes who came running toward the fence. The three dogs raced in the same direction, hackles raised, their frantic barking adding to the growing din.

Among the convergers were Doc Patrick and Judy Boyle, pushing their way roughly past those who had already reached the spot and were clustering near the fence. The Spring Hill Farm owner saw the two recumbent bodies and murmured, "Oh, my God!" but Doc said nothing and squeezed through the fence rails. He headed first for Frances Donovan.

Jane Gebhardt shook her head. "She's all right. Just fainted." She pointed. "It's Caleb!"

A twenty-year-old barn hand, Rob Fox, who had been among the first to reach the scene, was on his hands and knees beside the inert form. In thoughtless reaction, he had turned the boy over onto his back to get his face out of the dirt. Doc shouldered Rob aside and paled as he saw his young friend.

Caleb's eyes were half-open and glazed, tiny bits of earth clinging to the eyeballs and the mouth ajar. A single glance was all the vet required, but nevertheless he pressed three fingers to the carotid artery for a moment. He then ripped open the shirt and pressed his ear to the boy's bared chest. His expression was frozen as he looked up and met the fearful gaze of Judy Boyle crouched close by. There was utter finality in the single word he spoke to her.

"No."

Epilogue

D R. COLIN PATRICK MOVED SLOWLY, heavily, across the expansive ring to where the two horses, Royal Flush and Gay Blade, were tied side by side to the rail. Behind him people still milled near the fence. The blue roof lights of a McHenry County sheriff's car and the red lights of an orange and white van-type ambulance, both in the Spring Hill Farm lane, flashed ineffectually in the sunlight.

Close to the vehicles a mute knot of trainers and students stood watching unbelievingly as the cloth-covered, strapped-down body of Caleb Erikson was passed through the fence rails on a stretcher. A deputy was making notations as he talked with Judy Boyle, Jane Gebhardt and Frances Donovan. Colin Patrick himself had just finished speaking to the frightened red-haired girl and had patiently drawn from her a sobbed reconstruction of the events leading up to the tragedy. She had had little to offer. She had spoken to Caleb as she approached on Gay

Blade, but he hadn't answered. He hadn't even turned to look at her as the horse she was riding had passed and then stopped. He was just staring and she had thought he was looking toward the column of smoke from the hay fire in the back lot. No, he hadn't responded at all when she had spoken to him a second time. And then, for no reason she could fathom, her gelding had suddenly snorted and kicked and thrown her off. That was all she knew.

The veterinarian, as he always did, spoke softly, comfortingly to the two horses as he approached them. He walked directly to Gay Blade and let his hands pat the Anglo-Arab's neck and flank reassuringly. The gelding stood quietly as the familiar hands slid across withers and hip and rump, then down the leg, but he flinched and shied a little, partially lifting the left rear leg as the veterinarian's hands encountered the tender swelling just above the hock.

Doc nodded sadly, knowing now what had happened, sick inside at the needlessness of the tragedy and keenly mindful, as he had been on so many other occasions over the years, of the uncertainty of life. He straightened and returned to the front of the horse and let his gaze move from Gay Blade to Royal Flush and then back again.

"Caleb," he murmured, "you may be in there somewhere. You may be hearing me. From what the little girl said, you weren't inside yourself when it happened. You'd been watching Gay Blade's approach, so maybe you're inside him." He rubbed the gelding's satin-soft gray muzzle for a long quiet moment, then spoke again. "You may not be in either one. Maybe you saw something else — a bird or a rabbit. A dog, maybe."

He looked around briefly, but no one was near. Small

knots of people still clustered across the way by the fence and the emergency ambulance was beginning to back silently out of the lane. He looked back to the dapple-gray and spoke again, even more softly.

"If you're in there, Caleb, try to make Gay Blade do something to let me know. Make him cock an ear, Caleb."

Nothing.

"The tail, Caleb. Make him flick the tail."

Nothing.

"A sound, son. A nicker. If you're in there, make him nicker. *Please*."

Nothing.

Colin Patrick waited a long moment but there was no response whatever, neither from Gay Blade nor from Royal Flush, and at last he shook his head.

"I still think you're in there. Somewhere. You know what you've gone and done, don't you? No matter what animal I treat — or even see — from now on, I'll be wondering if you're there inside."

The rotund little veterinarian stood for fully a minute with his head bowed and his hand cupped over his eyes. Then he straightened and patted Gay Blade's neck a final time.

"Good-bye, Caleb."

Dr. Colin Patrick turned and walked back toward the others.

Through the large brown eyes of Gay Blade, the conscious-ness of Caleb Erikson watched the veterinarian walk away. He tried a final time, as he had been trying desperately ever since the man's approach, to force the gelding to re-act. He concentrated with all his power on making the horse nicker, but there was no response. The great fear that had been in his mind since the accident became even stronger. He had known at once that his own body was dead and he had continued sharing, albeit unwillingly, the experiences of Gay Blade as the gelding moved nervously to join Royal Flush. The two horses had walked together to the far corner of the exercise ring and stood there, apart from the frenzy of activity, comforted by one another's presence.

For Caleb, the fear was not so much inspired by the knowledge that his own body was dead. It arose more from the stunning realization that he could no longer transfer back into himself and the dawning suspicion that he was now sentenced to spend the remainder of his existence, such as it was, locked within the framework of a gentle Anglo-Arab dapple-gray.

He thought about trying to transfer his awareness into Royal Flush, but didn't make the attempt. His fear was too great. If he didn't try, then there was still the possibility, faint though it might be, that somehow he could do so. But if he tried and failed, then the certain knowledge that he was locked in this gelding for the rest of its life would be almost too much to bear.

Caleb Erikson had never been so afraid.

A barn hand had caught and tied the two horses side by side to the fence rail and when, after a period of time, the veterinarian approached, Caleb had watched through the horse's vision and felt a surge of hope. Doc knew of his unique talent and somehow Caleb might be able to give him a sign that the consciousness of the dead boy still existed. But then, after feeling the vet's careful hands on the gelding's side and hip and rump, after feeling the re-

newed pain that the touch of the vet's hand had caused to the wound left by the wasp, the fear became more intense.

With Gay Blade's vision he watched the familiar figure of the vet return to the front of the horse, felt his touch and heard through the gelding's ears with a welling of affection, the words of the man who was his friend. He strove mightily to make Gay Blade cock an ear or flick his tail as these requests were spoken aloud by the vet. Now he had failed in his last desperate attempt to cause Gay Blade to nicker, as Doc had asked.

With a terrible sense of despair, he watched from the dapple-gray as the short round man he had grown to love so much walked away. He yearned to scream, shout, stamp, whinny, do anything that would attract his attention and draw him back, but he was powerless to do anything but observe what the horse was looking at.

Was he really locked forever in this animal? He still existed. He was . . . and he knew he was! Did he have no more to look forward to from now on than to experience life through the senses of a gentle, plodding school horse? He longed to try to transfer his consciousness into something else, anything, but the fear that he would fail still bound him.

Across the lot, the people were gradually clearing away. The ambulance had already disappeared and the sheriff's car, along with another, was now driving off. The scattered people who remained moved into the barns until there were left behind only two small groups of people still talking to one another. A short, heavy-set man detached himself from one of these groups and walked to a white van parked near the office. Through Gay Blade's eyes, Caleb watched him climb inside and then the vehicle crunched over the graveled driveway, turned onto the highway and accelerated past where the dapple-gray stood tethered to the rail. Then it disappeared from view and an extended silence prevailed over the area.

A faint sound, stirring in its quality and quickly rising in volume, slipped into the silence and began filling it: a wild, exciting, musical crying from a multitude of throats. Both horses heard it and looked toward its source. The head of the dapple-gray known as Gay Blade was tilted upward and through the gelding's eyes Caleb saw the extensive ragged V of a flock of Canada geese, some two hundred strong, cleaving the sky like a gigantic wedge.

Of all the sounds in nature, there was none Caleb had ever liked more than the cries of wild geese. The sound had always stirred him mightily and it did so now. As he looked through Gay Blade's eyes at the birds, he willed himself toward the leader . . .

. . . and then his ears were filled with the clamor of suddenly close and very loud voices, including the one erupting joyously from his own throat. The goose he in-habited cocked his head and through his eyes Caleb saw, far below, a sprawling horse farm and, in one of the fenced lots, a black horse and a gray horse tied side by side.

And Caleb Erikson nearly burst with joy at the sure knowledge of his destiny.

Eckert
    Song of the wild

Rockingham Public Library
Harrisonburg, Virginia   22801

1. Books may be kept two weeks and may be renewed twice for the same period, unless reserved.

2. A fine is charged for each day a book is not returned according to the above rule. No book will be issued to any person incurring such a fine until it has been paid.

3. All injuries to books beyond reasonable wear and all losses shall be made good to the satisfaction of the Librarian.

4. Each borrower is held responsible for all books charged on his card and for all fines accruing on the same.